RESURRECTION MAN

"The real magic here is the tight focus and emotional intensity that Mr. Stewart sustains in tracking Dante's arduous journey." —*New York Times Book Review*

"Quite marvelous . . . It's not only the magic that fascinates in this novel. Stewart's descriptive details are finely chosen, making settings palpable; his characterizations are rich and imaginative . . . Stewart shows a true talent for inventive and intelligent fantasy." —*Publishers Weekly*

"Stewart's intuitive style infuses his latest novel with an artistry that demands attention." —*Library Journal*

"Absorbing and persuasive." —*Kirkus Reviews*

"Cleverly written . . . Stewart's controlled yet hauntingly poetic style gives this unusual plot something of the flavor of a mainstream family saga. Although his narrative weaves together threads of mystery, horror, and fantasy, Stewart's remarkable understated setting does a good job of showing us how both magic and altered history can serve as focusing lenses for the very real hopes and anxieties of believable people trying to learn to live with each other." —*Locus*

Ace Books by Sean Stewart

PASSION PLAY
NOBODY'S SON
RESURRECTION MAN

RESURRECTION MAN

SEAN STEWART

ACE BOOKS, NEW YORK

This Ace Book contains the complete text of the original hardcover and trade paperback editions.

RESURRECTION MAN

An Ace Book / published by arrangement with the author

PRINTING HISTORY
Ace hardcover and trade paperback editions / July 1995
Ace mass-market edition / June 1996

All rights reserved.
Copyright © 1995 by Sean Stewart.
Cover art by Tara McGovern.
This book may not be reproduced in whole or in part, by mimeograph or any other means, without permission. For information address: The Berkley Publishing Group, 200 Madison Avenue, New York, New York 10016.

The Putnam Berkley World Wide Web site address is
http://www.berkley.com

ISBN: 0-441-00339-7

ACE®
Ace Books are published by The Berkley Publishing Group,
200 Madison Avenue, New York, New York 10016.
ACE and the "A" design are trademarks
belonging to Charter Communications, Inc.

PRINTED IN THE UNITED STATES OF AMERICA

10 9 8 7 6 5 4 3 2

*For a spider I killed in Texas once,
and all my swallowed ghosts*

It is easy to go down into Hell; night and day, the gates of dark Death stand wide; but to climb back again, to retrace one's steps to the upper air—there's the rub, the task.

—VIRGIL

CHAPTER
ONE

DANTE STARED AND STARED AT THE CORPSE, BUT A blindness waited behind his eyes. It was as if he couldn't see the body; couldn't grasp it, or what it meant.

He had never felt fear like this, not in the worst moments of his life. The angel madness was thick in him, and with it came the inevitable dread: a metallic horror that slid like a sword down his throat. His skin crawled as if trying to escape; goose bumps sprang up in patches on his arms and neck and prickled uncontrollably across his face. His eyes were open but he couldn't see. His mouth tasted like oil.

What did it mean?

Christ.

What did it mean?

"O Jesus," he whispered. "Let's pretend it's all a bad dream, why don't we? Leave the damn thing here and go back to bed and hope it's gone by morning."

His foster-brother, Jet, grinned as Cain must have grinned at Abel. "Over your dead body," he said.

It wasn't the corpse of someone who looked like him, but Dante himself: he could see the tiny scar above the body's right eye where he had fallen into the stairs one Easter, hunting chocolate eggs. Just below the body's left elbow was the long white gash where a bucking saw-blade had cut into his arm one day when he and Jet were building their tree-fort. (Father had been out delivering a baby, so it was Mother who took over, swabbing the cut with mercurochrome and putting in the stitches, all fifty-three of them. Ought to save herself the trouble by running his arm through her sewing machine, she said, but she had been trained as a nurse and her fingers were steady.)

Even in the cold, the boathouse stank of mildew and engine oil and gutted fish. Jet and Sarah had rigged up an operating table, laying two-by-fours across the thwarts of the flat-bottomed rowboat. They had put Dante's corpse with its head in the stern, just touching the little Evinrude 2-stroke motor.

Jesus. What did it mean? That you're going to die, he told himself savagely. What do you think it foretells—a downturn in the economy? A low-pressure system bringing showers and scattered flurries? You're dying, dying, good as dead already and you know, you know it, some-how you can feel it coming somehow the angel's showing you O Christ Jesus—

He caught hold of himself.

Bad. Bad scientist, theorizing before all the data's in. Father would be disappointed (as usual). Examine the facts. Don't jump to conclusions. Lots of meanings for death symbols. Renewal. Sudden Change. Regeneration.

He looked again at his body, lying naked and pathetically vulnerable in the rowboat, with its feet hanging out over the prow. Renewal. Yeah, right.

In death, his pale skin was white as frost. His long white fingers looked sinister and strange. He imagined them creeping away, each hand a clumsy white spider crawling over the gunnels and dropping from the rowboat to scuttle out of sight, hiding behind the old oars and buckets of paint, the aluminum bait pails and fishing poles and disassembled Mercury outboard motor.

Dante's hair was a red-gold fringe around a high white forehead. He had his grandfather's ginger eyebrows, winging sharply up and out, like Satan's. The eyes below were narrow and blue. They stared unblinking at the naked boathouse bulb hanging overhead.

With a shaking hand Dante reached out and closed his own dead eyes.

Jet was papering the cold concrete floor with aging pages from *The New York Times,* in case things got messy. "You make a lovely corpse," he remarked. "I always thought you would."

"Pity Father isn't here to admire it," Dante muttered. (At the end of his worst nightmares, his father came with a scalpel to cut him open. The memory always stayed with Dante long after he woke: the long slide of the scalpel through his organs. The feel of his heart, throbbing, cupped in his father's careful hands.)

* * *

Strictly speaking, it was Jet who found the corpse. Dante had wanted no part of it.

But once the body was there, lying on his bedroom dresser, even Dante admitted they had to know where it had come from and what the hell it meant. If it was an omen as Jet pointed out, then they had better find out what the cause of death had been, so they could protect the real Dante from it. But of course they couldn't do an autopsy upstairs, even in the bathroom; Mother was a light sleeper and Father got up twice a night to pee. The boathouse, though cold and damp, was the only safe place. There they would have privacy and lots of water, plenty of pails and good light overhead.

It was after midnight. Smuggling the corpse out of the house had triggered in Dante a flood of childhood memories from a dozen other times when he and Jet and little Sarah had crept down the stairs at night, whispering and shushing one another, bumping into banisters in the dark and terrified they would wake their parents.

Quietly Dante's sister Sarah eased herself through the creaky boathouse door. In her right hand she carried an empty plastic ice-cream pail with a sponge, a pair of rubber gloves, and one of Aunt Sophie's butcher knives wedged next to a small hardcover book from Dad's study.

Sarah looked older than her twenty-eight years, Dante thought. Grim and running to fat. There was a time when he had played peek-a-boo with her, tickled her until her little round face turned red from laughing and her limbs went weak; a time when he had flown her like an airplane through the house, harrying Aunt Sophie and strafing the mortified cats.

"That didn't take long," he said.

"You were enjoying the wait?"

Getting on the wrong side of Sarah's tongue, as Jet had once observed, was like getting your face caught in a waffle iron.

Sarah studied her brother with eyes red from the crying she had done earlier, before she'd gotten herself under control. "You still want to go through with this?"

No! Dante started to say, but Jet cut him off. "We've got to know where the body came from. We've got to know what it means, and D's the only one who can tell us. He's the angel. He's the man with the talent for impossibilities."

"Well, I guess that's settled," Dante said lightly. He was amazed at how calm his voice sounded. How strange it was, to sit inside his own body and see it walk with his usual easy stride, hear it talk with his usual easy flippancy, too blind to see that his life had just been blown apart. Too numb to feel the angel waking in his midst.

But Dante felt it. He felt his heart running dry.

Chains snapping inside his chest.

The unfurling of terrible wings.

Jet picked the old book out of Sarah's ice-cream pail and flipped through its opening pages. "Miller's *Practical Pathology, Including Morbid Anatomy and Post-Mortem Technique.* Perfect." He adopted Father's Demonstration Voice, the one he used when examining specimens under the microscope or explaining horrible diseases. " 'Standing on the right side of the body, the pathologist grips his knife firmly with the right hand (Figure 1).' "

Jet grabbed an aluminum bait pail and flipped it over next to the rowboat so he could squat by the corpse. He glanced at Dante, his dark eyes sharp as obsidian. "Keep your grip firm!" he commanded. "You wouldn't want to make a mess now, would you? Not on this body."

Dante scowled. "Shut up."

"Yes, Master! It shall be as you desire," Jet wheezed, using Aunt Sophie's thickest Hungarian accent. Hunching his thin shoulders, he fussed at the body in the rowboat, smoothing its red-gold hair, pressing its arms neatly to its thin white flanks. He bobbed his head at Dante. "Your subject, Baron." A wicked grin flashed across Jet's face; lacy wings rose and fell on his right cheek.

It had been years since Dante had noticed Jet's butterfly birthmark, but now it fluttered before his angel's eyes, an evil portent. "Master's going to beat the shit out of Igor if Igor doesn't shut up."

(It was always this way with god damn Jet. "Like the two serpents around Hippocrates' staff," Father said once, chuckling. "All hiss and spit." . . . Easy to say if you weren't the one with Jet's venom in your eye.)

Dante swallowed. The hilt of Aunt Sophie's biggest butcher knife seemed to crawl like a wasp in his hand. "Okay," he said, licking his lips. "Okay."

"Shit—you must be scared." There was something like awe in Sarah's voice. "To risk getting bloodstains on your jacket!"

Dante blinked, then looked down. He was still wearing his favorite mandarin smoking jacket, the raw silk one with the wide lapels, wound about with dragons and steam. "Oh. Good point." He pulled it off, looking for someplace where it wouldn't get spotted with oil or old fish guts.

Perhaps it would be best if he slipped up to the house

to hang the jacket up. He could pour himself three fingers of Glenlivet to steady his nerves—

Sarah shattered his fantasy. "Here, give it to me. The girl's waiting and the condom's on, Casanova. It's time to perform."

Dante surrendered his jacket. Then, methodically, he removed his gold and garnet cuff links and put them in the pocket of his baggy black pants. He rolled up the sleeves of his rich brown dress shirt and pulled on the rubber gloves Sarah had pilfered from the kitchen.

Jet held up Miller's *Practical Pathology*. " 'Care must be taken not to go too deeply when incising the abdomen, in order to avoid cutting the liver or bowel,' " he recited.

"Does this excite you?" Sarah asked, turning on him. "Having you got some money riding on Dante's death, or are you just an asshole? I'm curious."

Sitting on his bucket by the rowboat, Jet went very still. His eyes were hooded and expressionless; his face was as white as the corpse beside him. "I didn't mean it to be like this."

Sarah's eyebrows rose. "Oh, really? I would have thought this would be perfect, Jet. Don't you just love scaring us shitless?"

Dante got his voice to work on the second try. "It's not his fault, Sarah." Didn't she understand that Jet was dying inside over his part in this? Didn't she know Jet loved Dante like his own breath?

Of course she didn't. Somehow Jet remained a stranger to everyone but him; and this house was only home for him when Dante was there.

Dante swallowed. God, he wished he were braver.

Why couldn't he be like Sarah or Mother or Aunt Sophie? Even Jet wouldn't be such a coward. "Jet just made
me look. The body is some kind of angel thing. It grew
on my dresser, it wears my face. It's some god damn
angel thing and I must have called it up. It's my responsibility." Once again Dante picked up Aunt Sophie's
knife. "It's my responsibility."

With a shaking hand Dante cut a line down the skin
of his own dead throat, feeling it split beneath his blade.

A spider crawled out through the crack and scuttled
around his neck, dropping out of sight.

Dante fainted.

As he fell he held on to one thought: this was his fault
for being wicked, for having used his madness. He had
let it out years ago, and now it was back to devour him.

Dante's magic first escaped on a playground when he
was six years old. Two henchmen were holding Jet down
while Duane the bully kicked him in the side. Jet was
flailing and screaming at Dante for help. Dante was crying and helpless, horribly afraid, but Duane and his buddies were Grade Threes. There was nothing he could do.

"Let's p-poke out his eyes," Duane suggested, looking
around for a stick.

Something in Dante gave way.

It was the strangest feeling, like a tent peg pulling out,
only deep inside. Something coming loose, water rushing,
and looking at Duane he smelled a horrible smell, hot
and dark and close, and heard a squeak, like a bedspring.
He saw Duane lying in the dark with his eyes wide open.

Vision spilled through Dante like hot water. His skin

crept and shivered and he felt sick to his stomach. "I'll tell," he shouted.

"Oh y-yeah? Tell what?" Duane jeered, flipping blond hair out of his round face.

Creak, creak. Creak, creak. A fan beating in the next room. The heat. "I'll—I'll tell Uncle you told on him," Dante shouted, not sure what he was saying.

The world stopped.

Dante's words went through Duane like bullets. "I n-never," he whispered.

Creak, creak. Dante smelt his fear like something cooking. Triumph rushed up in him, a flood of pure power because he hated Duane and now he *had him,* he could thread him like a worm on a hook. "Duane is a bad boy," he sang. "Duaney is a bad boy."

Because there was something, something in the dark room, in the heavy smell. "N-n-no," Duane said. "I d-I-I—" His stammer was back, so bad he couldn't talk. A wet stain crept across the front of his pants. *And Uncle sat beside him, and he closed his eyes, closed them hard,* and suddenly Dante didn't want to touch it anymore, but he couldn't stop seeing Duane's insides, as if he'd slit him open with one of his father's scalpels. Duane's buddies were staring at him, staring at the pee stain on his pants, but he just rocked back and forth, stammering, panic-stricken.

Terrified, Dante shook his head. There were spiders crawling in it. The madness was creeping through him, stinging him inside; his whole body curdled with poison. Frantically he tried to drag Duane's skin back over him.

A heavy weight settled over Duane—over Dante too—*and the dark air was hot and stank, and something stroked his leg, and he cried out.*

Duane turned and ran blindly for the school. His buddies exchanged looks and backed away from Dante.

Jet had stopped crying. His black eyes were still wet, the butterfly smeared with mud. Slowly he grinned at Dante, wiping his tear-stained face on the arm of his shirt. "Hey," he said. "Took you long enough."

That night Dante stood for hours before the mirror in his room, staring. From time to time, a spider would slide from between his lips, legs waving, and creep across his face.

He could not scream. He could not move.

How could he have known that a monster crouched inside him?

There was an angel buried in him; that much he figured out. It was terrible and could not be controlled. At six years old he knew it would split his father's head and eat his brains if Dante let it escape. It would tear off his mother's arms and drink her blood. He could never, ever, let it out.

It was impossible to ignore his talents, but it was easy to hide them. Once every two or three years all the kids in school would troop down to see his mom in the nurse's office to get their immunization shots and take their tests: color blindness, vocabulary, spatial manipulations, and the one the kids called the Angel Test. But the Angel Test was little more than a simple psychometry quiz: here's the object; which nurse had it last? We're going to put it behind one of these five screens; which screen is it behind? Easiest thing in the world to fail. Besides, psychometry wasn't one of Dante's strengths.

How could you devise a test for sneaking into someone's soul and freeing the wild animals there?

Some angels foresaw death. What school nurse wanted to hear a vision of her own ending?

Not Dante's mother. Once or twice, administering the Angel Test, she'd given him sharpish looks when maybe he'd gotten a few too many answers wrong. He guessed she was fudging his scores, and he knew that she had looked the other way when Duane's story, or ones like it, came to her ears. She did not want to lose her child to the angel's world of ghosts and visions. That was a comfort to him.

Father was different. He pushed Dante to use his gift— but rationally, for the common good. He thought of magic only as a tool, a potentially interesting new therapy yet to be perfected. He didn't understand about the madness.

He should have. It was Dante's father who taught him about God. "If there is a Deity, the one thing we can feel of Him is his savagery," Dr. Ratkay used to say.

Dante believed him.

"A two-dollar holding clamp shears; three hundred people die in an airplane crash. Are we really expected to believe in so monstrous a Divinity?"

Yes, yes! Dante would think. That's what it's like to be an angel, too. A bully lords it in the playground and an angel spears him like a worm on a hook.

But Father never understood.

Dr. Ratkay was a man of precise and definite tastes. He read only classical philosophers, drank only French wine, and listened only to German composers, except in certain frivolous moods when he might condescend to play a Hungarian—Liszt or Kodály.

Dr. Ratkay brought his children up as atheists, on moral grounds. "You know what they used to call the grave robbers who sold bits of dead bodies for research?" he would ask. "Resurrection Men, that's what. There's your Christ for you, my children. A Resurrection Man, making pennies off a bag of old bones. 'Neither fear your death's day, nor long for it,' as Martial says. If there is a God, don't give Him the satisfaction. If there is a God, He is more than harps and grace and candlelight.

"God hissed through the vents at Auschwitz," Dante's father used to say.

God creeps on eight thin legs.

YOU ARE OBSTINATE, PLIANT, MERRY, MOROSE,
ALL AT ONCE. FOR ME THERE'S NO LIVING
WITH YOU, OR WITHOUT YOU. —MARTIAL

CHAPTER
TWO

IT WAS ALWAYS THE TWO OF THEM. DANTE QUICK AND
laughing, Dante the lead in the school play, Dante and
the girls, Dante, Dante: his smile, golden. His touch,
magic.

. . . And Jet always behind him, thin and dark as a
shadow. Watching. Hardly real, the neighbors murmured
to one another, glancing at the butterfly on his cheek.
Already marked for some strange destiny.

Only Dante was close enough to bully him, needle him,
swap comic books, catch him crying at the end of *Char-
lotte's Web*. They grew up like twins together; to the rest
of their little community on the outskirts of the city Jet
was insubstantial, but to Dante he was always real
enough to touch. He had felt Jet's wiry strength when

they wrestled in the grass; tasted Jet's blood when they swore their brotherhood. Jet had saved his life.

Of course that was only fair, after that day on the playground when Dante had lost his soul to save Jet's eyes.

The first time Jet saved his life it was 1969.

Minotaurs were stalking Watts and Harlem in broad daylight. On the bright side, the oracle who had tried to save JFK was taken seriously enough to thwart an assassination attempt on Robert Kennedy. The United States and China, in a rare show of superpower responsibility, had brokered a peaceful settlement to the conflict in Vietnam, though ugly wars still burned in Georgia and Turkmenistan. Five thousand lottery families had settled into Perfect, U.S.A., but they still weren't getting the same kinds of health and productivity stats the Chinese routinely reported from the Permitted City, and the Administration was said to be looking for a different project to restore American prestige. Rumors abounded. Social activists clamored for the allocation of Great Society money to rebuild the Philadelphia slums, or integrate Indian and white cultures in the Great Plains.

But President Kennedy was said to favor a return to good old Yankee know-how. He wanted a monorail grid, an orbital satellite, or maybe the creation of a government-directed research effort to capitalize on the new superconducting ceramics coming out of M.I.T.'s Materials Tech Division.

In November of that year Aunt Sophie's coins foretold a harsh winter.

Dante was breezing through Grade 5. It had been

almost two years since he had last felt the angel in him stir and flex its wings. When he thought of magic, he thought of *Dr. Strange* and the Children's Rescue Society and *I Dream of Jeannie.*

The river at the bottom of the garden rarely froze before Christmas, but just as Aunt Sophie had predicted, November ended with two weeks of hard cold. By the first of December ice stretched almost to the middle of the channel.

Jet always said it was Dante who made the dare. Certainly it was Dante who left Sarah watching *Gilligan's Island* under strict orders not to leave the parlor. The boys snuck down to the river and it was Jet who went first, walking with his customary strange certainty, seven steps out onto the frozen surface and seven steps back.

Then it was Dante's turn.

It was half past four, but already the sun had slipped below the edge of the river valley. The air was as dim and heavy as Aunt Sophie's leaded crystal. Dante's breath smoked in the cold. Jet's didn't.

Dante took a step out onto the ice. Near the bank it was white like frost, but over the channel it was the same murky blue as the sky. He walked out a little farther, trying to step in Jet's bootprints, knowing Jet's instincts would be better than his.

On his fifth step, the ice creaked with a sound like wooden floorboards, only crisper. Dante stopped. Smoke curled from his mouth. (He imagined a winter palace, lit with candles of ice that threw off cold blue light and coils of white vapor.)

On his sixth step he felt the ice shiver under his feet. The creaking was louder. (The light would come from the souls of little boys, one trapped inside each icicle. When a candle burned down to nothing, the boy inside would be gone forever.)

Here the bank dropped sharply to a deep channel. If he felt the ice start to go he would have to throw himself back to the bank. If he went through he might get lucky and be able to touch bottom.

The ice groaned and shuddered underfoot.

Carefully Dante turned his head.

"You can back out," Jet said. The butterfly clung to his pale face. It could have been resting on a scrawny snowman with coal-black eyes.

Jet knew Dante was going to go through: suddenly this was very clear to both of them. He had led Dante out to the exact place where he would fall in and die. Dante would drown and Jet would have everything to himself: Dante's house, Dante's parents, Dante's room and comic books and chemistry set and toboggan. It was so obvious, Dante wondered why he had never seen it before: Jet wanted him to die.

His left foot went through as he tried to turn around. He lurched back. Another plate of ice gave beneath his thigh. He yelled and twisted onto his front. More ice gave way. He was through to his hips, lying on his chest with his hands splayed out, reaching for the bank.

Jet turned and ran.

Dante screamed and clawed the ice, trying to drag himself up, but there was nothing to grab and his legs were heavy as iron. His muscles cramped in the unbelievable cold and his legs were two iron posts tied to his waist, pulling him into the black water. He had always imagined the river was still when the ice closed over it, but the current was murderous, dragging at his useless legs.

He was going to drown. They would pull his white body out of the river and his father would weep as he sliced him open.

And then Jet was flying down the riverbank, great stumbling strides, dragging an oar he must have pulled from the boathouse. Dante grabbed the wide flat blade and Jet, lying with his stomach on the ice, pulled with all his strength. Dante wriggled forward like a fish, working his hips back onto the ice, then his thighs, then churning and splashing to shore.

Shivering and crying uncontrollably, he let Jet lead him up to the house. Mother, taking in his sniffles and his waterlogged clothes in a glance, sent him off to the bathtub, tight-lipped with fury. All the time he lay in the tub he could hear her hammering away at Jet, but Jet never said whose idea it had been to go out on the river.

" 'Of all the animals, the Boy is the most unmanageable,' " Father said at the dinner table that night. He glanced approvingly at Jet. "Good thought, to fetch that oar. If you'd reached out for my silly son here with your hand, you'd have gone in yourself. It happened six or seven years ago over in Millerton: five people drowned one after another, each one trying to pull the last one out. But for once, the fool seems to have profited from the wise man, Cato notwithstanding. I'm surprised you thought of the oar in time."

"It was easy," Jet said. He shot Dante a look, half-mocking, half-merry. "I knew he was going to fall in."

From that moment, Dante knew he hadn't imagined the hunger in Jet's eyes as he fell through the ice. Jet had saved his life, that was true. But as the years went by, time only added to Dante's belief that a part of Jet was always watching him, waiting for him to die.

They dared one another often.

Dante dared Jet to jump from the big willow on Three Hawk Island straight into the river; dared him to pinch the latest *X-Men* from Percy's Store; dared him to eat Aunt Sophie's schnitzel after covering it in chocolate sauce (which he did), and dared him to sneak downstairs after the grown-ups were asleep, take the tall bottle of Glenlivet from the liquor cabinet, and drink a brandy snifter full of it in under five minutes, which he also did, with his eyes watering in pain and his thin body racked with suppressed coughs.

In turn, Jet dared Dante to steal one of Aunt Sophie's coins, to walk widdershins around the Pentecostal church by the school, and, in the aftermath of the Glenlivet episode, to smoke Father's pipe.

Only Dante's pride kept him from funking on this one. Father kept his pipes in a mug on top of his desk; also dangling from the edge of the mug, like an insect crawling from its depths, was the old fishing lure that only Dante knew was one of the three magic things in the house. (The others were Grandfather Clock and the mirror on Dante's bureau, where many years later Jet would force him to look at his own dead body.)

The desk was scary enough without the lure. Dr. Ratkay kept a skull on it, for starters; to keep him humble, he said. Jet had once dared Dante to put his fingers through its eyeholes.

Beside the skull sat the old leather scalpel case. It was just like the velvet-lined box Aunt Sophie kept the family silver in. Four knives and four pairs of surgical scissors waited inside, gleaming against the red velvet interior. One scalpel in particular, the second largest, held a special horror for Dante: his father always brought it with him when he came into Dante's dreams.

But at some level Dante knew the skull was only polished bone, the scalpels sharpened steel; each wrapped in coils of his own fear. He knew that. Even the dreaded Gray's *Anatomy* wouldn't hurt him if he didn't open the pages, or meet the hollow eyes of the Skinned Man on its cover.

The lure was different. It had three segments, like a steel wasp: a small rounded head, a teardrop thorax, and a curving tail. Thin barbed hooks dangled from it like legs and it held its own madness, its own venomous sting.

Goaded on by Jet's needling, Dante had finally snatched a pipe from the mug, keeping his hand well away from the lure. He lit the pipe with trembling fingers, inhaled and then hacked desperately around the hand Jet had clapped over his mouth to quiet him. It was no good: the alarm had been raised, and they couldn't disguise the smell before Father marched downstairs to administer what turned out to be the last spanking Dante ever got.

Dante never touched the pipe again, but it wasn't the fear of a whipping that kept him away, or the choking memory of the smoke. It was the horrible presence of the lure, crawling like a wasp from between the pipes.

Dante had been unable to get the lure out of his mind for some time before the Thanksgiving visit that brought him home to discover his own dead body. For weeks he had seen it every night as sleep welled up and set his mind drifting. It winked and glittered dimly before him as if twisting through dark water, and he followed it into deeps of dreaming. . . .

And so like a fool, never imagining it would lead to finding his own dead body less than twenty-four hours later, he picked it up at last. He knew it was madness, but he was tired of being afraid, tired of the sight of the lure in his dreams every night, glinting and glimmering. Fishing with it by day, he reasoned, would be like flipping on the bedroom light to prove there were no monsters crouching underneath the bed.

So easily it hooked him.

He took off from the lab a day early and drove home on the Wednesday before Thanksgiving. In the gray dark before the next dawn, heart hammering, he unhooked the lure from the pipe mug on his father's desk and slipped outside into a cold morning.

When the hook caught his hand on the first cast, he should have taken the hint. He should never have sucked his finger and swore and sent the lure spinning into the river with a smear of his red blood on it.

The lure gleamed and guttered in a river dark as sleep; guttered and gleamed like a cold steel candleflame.

A doomed pike snapped it up.

After a hard fight Dante landed the brute. Scooping it into a net, he got a firm grip on its tail and slammed its head into the concrete piling at the end of the dock. The pike stiffened. Shudders raced along its body.

Dante closed his eyes.

He slammed the fish into the piling again. It arched,

more slowly this time. Tiny shudders ran along its back. It lay still.

Dante shivered. His hands were cold and slimy, and stank when he blew on them. It was only a fish, he told himself. An old fat river pike, two and a half feet long. Sewage-colored. He picked it up by the tail. Water dripped from its mouth, and a little blood, spotting the dock. Dante walked back to the filleting table by the boathouse.

(And the exact slimy feel and the precise dank stink of this fish rushed over his senses and filled him up with echoes of hundreds of other fish he had caught here, a lifetime of jiggering hooks out of their stiff lips, of avoiding their accusing eyes.)

Dante caught his breath.

Holding the pike upside down, he picked up a knife and started cleaning it. Pike scales showered onto the table, fingernail-sized, fan-shaped. Dante remembered his father with a pocket magnifying glass, showing him how you could count scale-rings to tell how old a fish was, as if it were a tree.

"Every part of the cadaver is instructive," Dante muttered. "As Father used to say." He wondered what he would find.

A broad flat light was spreading in the sky.

Nothing. He wouldn't find anything.

He made a long incision along the pike's back, following the spine. The mottled skin split, showing transparent flesh below. Next, two perpendicular cuts just below the head, one on each side of the backbone. Then slowly he peeled the flesh back, digging delicately at any clinging meat to expose the spinal column and the ribs.

Father would be proud.

Flipping the fish over, Dante cut off the fins and slit its belly open. The viscera slid out in a pool of blood. Carefully Dante dissected the bladder, liver, heart.

Inside the stomach, a clutch of shapeless half-digested minnows, the remnants of two small perch, and a curiosity: another pike, a little one half the length of his hand, and so fresh he could have cleaned and served it too. It couldn't have been swallowed more than an hour before Dante had avenged its murder.

Delicately Dante took out the smaller fish, and began a second autopsy.

In its belly he found a square golden ring. It could have been a man's thick wedding band, though Dante could not remember having seen a square ring before. With the tip of his knife he pulled it clear of the viscera and studied it in the broadening daylight.

Aunt Sophie was in the kitchen, brewing a cup of willow-bark tea, when Dante returned to the house. When he showed her the ring she screamed and fainted. Later, when Mother brought her around, Aunt Sophie swore and coughed and lit a cigarette with shaking fingers, but she would not speak to Dante, or look at the strange square ring.

At dinner they pretended nothing had happened. The silences were excruciating. For Dante it was like being a child again, fidgeting while grown-up secrets filled the air.

At first it looked like Sophie wouldn't be able to cook, after the shock Dante had unwittingly given her, but after a short rest upstairs—they could hear the clink and clatter of her coins—she decided to return to the kitchen, and prowled it, scowling, for the rest of the afternoon, vengefully slicing vegetables and hammering her meat into mute submission.

Beef broth came first, salty and black as blood. Countless afternoons Dante had helped her make it, chopping vegetables and fussing with seasoning, until at four o'clock she would scoop up the bones in her big wooden ladle and fish out the marrow for them to spread on toast and eat. For a proper broth all the vegetables came out just before serving, making two tureens: one black bouillon with noodles in it, the other beef-stained potatoes and onions and carrots, and peppers slathered with so much horseradish that eating them was like having your sinuses dosed with ammonia.

Jet scooped potatoes onto his plate. "So they shot a minotaur in Westwood Heights yesterday."

"Westwood Heights!" The little worry lines in Mother's white forehead deepened and she couldn't help glancing at Dante. "I thought those things only haunted The Scrubs, or maybe Peter Street."

"Extra, Extra: Minotaurs manifest outside the slums." Jet shrugged. "The magic's rising all the time. Who knows what brought it on—fear of Volvos? I don't know. I shot some pictures for the paper."

"Maybe the Mammon Men have oracled a stock crash coming," Sarah suggested. "How many people did it get?"

Jet helped himself to some peppers and horseradish. "One family and a paper boy, plus two more injured. It was a slasher: standard dark figure with a knife. When they shot it, it was wearing the face of its last victim."

Dante shuddered, not sure whether Jet meant the min-otaur had flayed one of the people it had killed and made a mask of the skin, or whether, governed by the strange dream-logic that drove such manifestations, the monster always appeared as its victim's twin. Both possibilities seemed equally horrible.

"But still. You would never have seen that five years ago." Mother's small head shook in crisp disapproval. Dante noticed that her gorgeous hair, once red as fire, was now embering into ashes. Guiltily he wondered when that had happened, and why he hadn't noticed un-til now.

"Oh, it's clearly getting worse, there's no doubt about that," Father said, filling Mother's wineglass with a nice French white from the mid-eighties. "I remember when we first started hearing of this sort of thing—at the end of the War, when they liberated the concentration camps."

"The Golem of Treblinka," Jet said.

Father filled his glass. "There was one at Dachau too: killed two hundred prisoners and four guards, and they never shot it down." He moved around the table, pouring for Sarah and Aunt Sophie. "Now, what's needed is a scientist with some aptitude for this angel business to make a thorough study of the phenomenon." He paused, standing over Dante's shoulder. "There are tremendous contributions to be made. The man who learns enough to banish these manifestations, or better still stop their formation, will be the Pasteur or the Fleming of his time." He emptied the bottle deliberately into Dante's glass.

"Hurrah for that unknown savior," Dante said.

Mother looked at Dante sharply, her hand hovering over a dish of honey-ginger carrots. "Don't you go looking for trouble."

Father returned to his place at the head of the table. " 'But the bravest surely are those who have the clearest vision of what is before them, glory and danger alike, and yet notwithstanding go out to meet it'—Thucydides."

"And after all, what are his alternatives?" Jet mused, ignoring Dante's glare. "He certainly doesn't *apply* himself to anything else— Was it not Hippocrates who said, 'Idleness and lack of occupation tend—nay, are dragged!—towards evil!' "

Dr. Ratkay scowled.

Sarah ladled black broth into her bowl. "Parody is the sincerest form of flattery," she observed, smirking at her father.

Aunt Sophie snorted over her wine, her smoke-blue eyes angry, her old hand trembling around the stem of her glass. "Dante get hurt playing Angel? Pfeh! Dante couldn't make a living reading tea leaves."

A honey-ginger genie steamed up over the table as Mother took the lid off the carrots. "That's like saying he's not a good enough shot to blow his own head off," she said tartly.

"Thanks for the vote of confidence, Mom."

"Point and set to Mother," said Sarah, who kept score of such things.

After soup and vegetables came a tray of roasted peppers stuffed with spiced beef and rice. In the middle of the table, proud as the head of John the Baptist on its silver platter, a mountain of wienerschnitzel loomed: veal on one side and pork chops on the other, breaded and fried in lard, golden-brown and glistening.

"The American Medical Association estimates that each schnitzel takes five minutes off your life," Sarah remarked, helping herself to two of the veal.

"Not if you don't inhale," Jet countered. "And don't believe everything you read about the dangers of second-hand schnitzel either."

"More self-serving lies from the lackeys of the schnitzel industry," Sarah retorted, shaking her head. She looked appealingly to Father at the head of the table. "Tell him, Doctor!"

A piece of veal impaled on his fork, Dr. Ratkay paused. "Tragic," he said solemnly. "The arteries harden, the belt line disappears. The human waste of it!"

They groaned as he patted his waist, where a small pot belly distended his shirt-front.

"I could quit any time I wanted," Dante said, mouth half full. "Look—I'm under a lot of stress at the lab. A couple of schnitzels calm me down. Is that so wrong?"

Jet cut his schnitzel from the bone, cut the fat from the schnitzel, dissected out a precise, bite-sized morsel and placed it in his mouth. "Oh, hey," he said. "Menthol."

"Pfeh! When I was young, every day we eat for breakfast a slab of bacon fat between two slices of lard," Aunt Sophie said, in a strong Hungarian accent. She pointed proudly to her own arms, still sturdy after seventy years. "You think I get from bran flakes and skim milk so strong?"

Aunt Sophie hadn't lived in Hungary since 1929, though she visited when she could. She spoke perfect English, and swore perfect American.

She lifted a slab of schnitzel, golden and gleaming, and snorted, scoffing at her little brother and his medical degree. "To hell with you," she said.

Aunt Sophie's Hell was a very definite place. Growing up, Dante was sure that she remembered each thing she had consigned there, why she sent it and where it lay.

Aunt Sophie was odd, even for a grown-up. Two packs of Virginia Slims a day had turned her eyes the color of cigarette smoke; as a boy, Dante always felt their fire in her, smoldering. She cooked strange things, like bread fried in lard, and ate them at strange times, like five in the morning or three in the afternoon. Dante once found her at the kitchen table at two A.M., still dressed, frowning at a pattern her magic silver dollars had made while she sipped a mug of fennel-seed tea and ate tiny pickled onion, one after another. She had lived with them forever, and loved Dante dearly, but she never came to his birthday parties, not even once.

She was also the first grown-up he could remember hearing swear. He was seven at the time; her hair was still long and straight and black, her fingers thin and yellow at the tips.

The City had not crept up to the edges of their community then; the kids still went to a country school that served all grades. It was early spring, and Dante had trudged home from the bus stop half a mile through the slush, carrying a strange truth inside himself. A Grade 11 named Jason Babych had died. Something to do with a girl, Jet said. Got up before dawn and shot himself behind the family barn. His dad had found him there.

How Jet knew these things Dante never understood,

or even questioned. Jet was awake in a way other kids were not. He understood the grown-ups' codes and ciphers; he read the secrets behind their looks and hesitations as Dr. Ratkay read Parkinson's in the tremor of an old man's hand, or heard the rot in people's lungs when they coughed.

What Jet found out he told Dante, forcing him to share the unclean knowledge. One of Dante's clearest childhood memories was the feel of the secrets Jet thrust on him: sinister things, heavy with obscure adult meanings.

The Grade 11 dead, slumped against his father's barn. Something to do with a girl.

Knowing about it made Dante feel dirty. He wanted to talk to someone, someone who wasn't Jet.

Mother would be angry that he knew. She worked at the school. She probably knew Jason Babych, Dante realized.

They would have called Father. He might already have cut into Jason's dead body with one of his scalpels, only it wouldn't hurt, because Jason was dead.

So Dante found Aunt Sophie and moped, and let her make him a piece of toast, and told her, and waited for her to do a magic trick or tell a funny story that would make him feel better.

She didn't. "Bloody fool," she said angrily. "Hah! . . . I bet Jet told you that, didn't he?"

Dante didn't answer.

"Of course he did. Little spy." Angrily she filled the kettle for tea and banged it onto the stove. She was still strong then, very strong. "I'll tell you what, that boy was a fool, a coward and a fool. To kill yourself—that's the one most contemptible thing you can do. Remember that! It's stupid and it's disrespectful. He's a coward that does that. Can't stomach the hard going, that's all it is. . . . A coward and a traitor, that's what he was, the bastard," she finished, so fiercely Dante started to cry.

She wasn't seeing him, though; Aunt Sophie was staring at something far in the distance, or the past. "To hell with him," she said at last. "To hell with him."

CHAPTER
THREE

THE SPIDER THAT HAD CRAWLED FROM DANTE'S neck was gone.

Swimming back to consciousness, he found himself sitting on an overturned bait pail. Jet was squatting next to him, propping him up, with one hand on his shoulder. Something was hanging just over Dante's head. He realized it was his own dead foot, sticking out beyond the end of the rowboat.

This right here is a pretty good approximation of Hell, Dante reflected. He glanced over at Jet: bastard Jet who had found the damn body beneath the bureau mirror. "Little spy" was right.

Sarah brought him a mug of water from the boathouse sink. It tasted cool and metallic. "Are you going to be

31

able to do this? Because I can try—"

Dante shook his head. He frowned at his slacks, brushing off imaginary lint to steady his nerves. "Mine to do."

"You sure?"

Slowly Dante stood. He picked up the butcher knife and gave Sarah his best wry smile. "Cross my heart and hope to die."

With death, the blood had pooled on the underside of his body, giving a heavy, bruised look to the backs of his knees, thighs, back and neck.

Dante cut, and cut again.

The dead look nothing like the sleeping, he thought. Many times he had been moved by the vulnerability of a sleeping lover, the fragile innocence of a woman's mouth half-open like a child's. There was nothing innocent about death. The body that split heavily around his knife wasn't him anymore. It had become a thing: nothing more than what his godless father saw, a blind and purposeless machine, now broken and useless. There could be no more complete degradation.

Jet read on from Miller's *Practical Pathology*. " 'The next step in the process is the dissection of the skin and muscles of the chest from sternum, cartilages, and ribs, and, at the same time, of the skin of the neck from the subjacent tissue. This should be done by grasping the skin, et cetera, with the left hand—' "

"The skin, et cetera," Dante murmured. "Dear God."

Jet's thick black eyebrows rose in reproof. Still doing his unnervingly good imitation of Dr. Ratkay's Demonstration Voice, he resumed reading. " '—grasping the skin, et cetera, with the left hand and steadily pulling away from the sternum or ribs. The areolar tissues are then touched here and there with the edge of the knife as they are put upon the stretch.' " Jet glanced up. "Just like filleting a fish," he said.

" 'Commencing at the second costal cartilage close to its attachment to the rib, and cutting obliquely outwards, so as to avoid injuring the underlying lung, one divides the cartilages on either side.' "

Dante's hands were sweating inside their rubber gloves. Carefully he sawed through his own cartilage.

" 'Great care should be taken not to splinter the ribs in any way, so as to avoid puncture wounds of the hands in subsequent manipulations. An excellent way to avoid such wounds is to fold the skin which has been dissected from sternum and ribs in over the severed ends of the ribs,' " Jet read.

Dante felt like crying. Why had he gone fishing with the accursed lure? (Could that only have been this morning? It seemed like a lifetime ago—which it was, he thought, with a quick flash of bitter humor.) Was he meant to find the strange square ring? What did it signify? Clearly Aunt Sophie recognized it, or thought she did.

Why, why had he ever let Jet near the mirror?

Dante was twenty-one when the mirror overmastered him. He was home from college for Christmas, and hating it. In the City he was still a stranger to his impersonal apartment, living on the surface of things. He liked it that way.

But at home . . . The old house crawled with his childhood secrets, and he had lost the trick of ignoring them.

The mirror was the worst of all. The antique bureau

it ornamented was a long mahogany monster that drank Aker's Lemon Furniture Oil by the quart. It had a facing of white Italian marble with black streaks through it, like fudge-ripple ice cream. A three-foot-high oval mirror rose from its center. The glass around the mirror's edges had been frosted, like ice ringing a pond in winter.

This was the mirror that had stood in judgment over Dante the day he poisoned Duane the bully with unclean secrets. He had watched spiders crawl from his mouth in its remorseless depths. Over the years the dread of it had grown in him. One night he heard its icy surface creak; felt it shift under the weight of his eyes. He snatched up an old bedspread and flung it over the mirror before he fell through the cracking glass into whatever black river waited below.

Since that time Dante had not dared to touch the bureau, letting it go dry and parched for lack of oil. He hated looking at it, and seldom came home anymore, because it meant spending a night in the same room as the cursed thing. And every time he did come back, he could not help noticing a shape growing beneath the bedspread.

Something solid was growing under the blanket. Something was waiting for him in the mirror's depths.

It finally caught him after dinner that night. He had snuck back to his room; Jet and Sarah found him sitting on the edge of his bed, staring at the strange square ring and trying to think up some excuse for spending the night on the couch in the parlor.

"What happened with Aunt Sophie?" Sarah asked.

"She's bolted the door to her room. From the smell of it, she's trying to fumigate the place with a carton of Virginia Slims Queen-size."

"Dante wants to earn his wings and halo," Jet drawled. "Going to try his hand at angeling at last."

"To hell with you. Aunt Sophie can have her secrets; I don't want any part of them."

"What do you suppose happened to her husband?" Jet mused. "Or the baby?"

"He died a long time— Baby?" Dante's gingery eyebrows flared up in surprise. "What baby?"

"I . . . found a picture of them, Aunt Sophie and your mother. Both very pregnant."

"Found a picture? Where?"

"Can't remember."

"You remember everything," Dante said suspiciously. "What happened to Aunt Sophie's baby, Dante?"

"How should I know? Miscarried, I suppose, or stillborn. That's enough reason not to talk about it." Dante shrugged, pushing away another one of Jet's unpleasant secrets. "What are you digging for? That should be horrible enough."

"Why doesn't she come to your birthday parties? Hey?" Jet grinned, and the butterfly trembled on his cheek. "What's that little ring you found, that least of rings? What did Aunt Sophie see in the depths of its golden eye, eh?" He steepled his fingers in monkish solemnity. "You cannot hide from Fate, my son."

Sarah grunted. "People don't have fates."

"No: fates have people," Jet said, suddenly serious. "It's quite, quite different."

Dante blinked, caught by Jet's stare. Unbidden, the

thought popped into his mind: Jet. Jet is my fate. He has me.

"What happened to the father?" Sarah asked, not noticing the long look that hung between her brothers. "Aunt Sophie's husband, that is. She would never have a baby without being married, but she never wears a ring."

"A ring," Dante whispered, reaching into his pocket. It was still there, a thick, square gold band. Unornamented. Like a man's wedding ring.

"We'll get you your crystal ball license yet," Jet purred.

Sarah frowned. "If you found her husband's wedding ring in the river, maybe he drowned. Maybe he and the baby were drowned on the same day—on your *birthday*, Dante! That would explain why she never comes to your parties. She's at a cemetery or something."

"What's the first thing you remember?" Jet murmured. "The very earliest memory you have?"

"I don't know. Grandfather Clock, I guess. I could see my reflection in his front. I remember the ticking." Dante turned the ring over in his hand. The gold was a heavy, metallic yellow, the same color as his cuff links.

Jet said, "I remember everything." Sarah snorted but he ignored her, looking only at Dante, his black eyes fierce above a thin smile. "The first time I woke, you were seven days old. I know; I heard Aunt Sophie and your mother talking about it in the next room. I understood them perfectly."

Dante believed him.

"It was your crying that woke me," Jet continued, sitting on the bureau, his legs idly swinging. His hand rested on a lump under the bedspread. "I was lying in a basket on the kitchen table, beside an open window. You were lying beside me. They must have heard your whimpers; Mother sighed and came into the room. Her footsteps were slow and painful. Aunt Sophie followed her.

"Your mother picked you up and held you, singing, looking out the window to the river. She was young then, younger than Sarah is now." Jet grinned. "Prettier too."

Was it Jet who told you that? Aunt Sophie had asked. *Of course it was, the little spy.* . . . The most contemptible thing there is. He was a coward and a traitor, Aunt Sophie had said. Who? Who was the traitor she had been thinking of that day, as her eyes stared back into the past?

Dante fingered the ring. A man's wedding ring.

Jet's voice was soft. "Then Mother looked at me, and the singing died in her throat. 'Sophie,' she whispered. The next thing I saw was Aunt Sophie's face bending down. Do you understand? *I was the baby, Dante.* I was Aunt Sophie's child."

Sarah shook her head. "We would have known."

Jet ignored her, looking only at Dante, always at Dante. "She saw me and she screamed. She screamed and screamed and wouldn't stop screaming. . . . She has never stopped screaming. I hear it all day long between the ticks of Grandfather Clock, Dante. The whole house rings with it. The walls shudder."

Jet closed his eyes. "What happened to the baby, eh?" When he opened them again, Dante's heart stopped beating, so naked was Jet's rage. "*What happened to me?* You were Mother's child and I was Aunt Sophie's, only something happened to me when I was one week old. Something put *this* on me," he said, reaching up to finger the butterfly birthmark. "Something made me inhuman,

Dante. Something took me out of the sunlight to be your god damn shadow.

"For years I didn't care, that's just the way it was, I grew up the outsider, who ever thought different? But that's not enough anymore. Now I want to know, Dante. I want to know what happened."

Dante said, "I can't tell you that."

Jet jumped off the bureau with a tight laugh, tense with fury. "You're an angel, damn it! You can find out."

"I can't. I don't know how."

"Well *learn!*" And with a savage jerk, Jet yanked the bedspread off Dante's bureau to leave the white marble top bare.

Dante's body lay under the mirror's cold unblinking eye. He was dead.

Dante couldn't scream. He couldn't move.

Helpless, he stared into the mirror. Helpless, he saw himself bending over the corpse. Only he was wearing his father's face, and he held a scalpel in his hand.

"The autopsy is like the third movement of a sonata," his father once said. "The Body; the Life; the Body Reconsidered."

Dante reconsidered himself, lying dead and mutilated in the boathouse. An autopsy is all about time, he thought. Alive we stand against the stream and hold our shape; dead, we drift with the current, carried from the land of the living and lost at last even to memory.

Holding the tissue apart with the thumb and index finger of his left hand, he peered down into his own dead abdomen at a white, fibrous sac, of the sort spiders fill with their eggs. It was half the size of a football, engulfing most of his liver and half a kidney.

"Dear God," Sarah whispered. She grabbed for a bait pail and retched.

Standing beside Dante, Jet reached down with one finger to touch the sac, ever so gently. "Still warm," he said.

Hands shaking, Dante stripped off his rubber gloves and looked away from the white sac growing in his body cavity. He could feel the growth inside him now, a sticky alien mass webbed around his vital organs. Threads of it like cobweb tangling his heart.

He didn't want to die. Not yet. Please, God.

The sudden blank uselessness of his life yawned under him like a pit. Thirty-one years old and what had he done? Nothing. Never finished his degree, never fell in love.

Oh, he had felt affection for women—lots of women. But love? Love was something else again. What he felt for Jet and Sarah, Mom and Dad and Aunt Sophie, was not an emotion, but a fact: something as real as a stone.

He had never let a woman get that close to him. He had never made a family of his own. Never would.

He glanced at Sarah, twenty-eight and smart and grown, and saw buried in her his baby sister: a chubby toddler gone missing, he and Jet the frantic babysitters running like madmen up and down the river trails for half an hour before Dante saw her at last, pelting down a path and laughing and waving her diaper overhead like the banner of a victorious legion.

Sarah had stopped retching. She took a long moment to steady her nerves, and then forced herself to consider the body in the boat. A humorless smile flickered across her mouth. "Was it not Socrates who said, 'The unexamined death is not worth dying'?"

Dante's heart hammered endlessly inside his chest. Up the hill, Grandfather Clock would still be ticking in the parlor, long after the last ember in the fireplace had smoked and died. Mother and Father would be lying in their twin beds; Aunt Sophie would be dreaming her unquiet dreams of crows and cigarettes.

Sarah studied the white growth in the dead Dante's abdomen. "Maybe Dad can cut it out. If there's one of these in you, I mean."

A nightmare image raced through Dante: his father, bending over him, slitting him open. The slide of the knife through his organs. His heart, beating in his father's hands.

Dante shook his head. "It's got its hooks into too many vital systems. Liver. Kidneys. Spleen maybe. Heart maybe. It's too late for surgery." Dante shuddered, feeling the barbed world biting into him with thin, evil little hooks.

"What do we do with the body?" Sarah asked.

"Let's burn it," Dante said. "Burn the sac and the body both. Burn everything. Then I'll drink myself into a coma," he added. "Fabulous idea."

Sarah ignored him. "We can't toss it in the river. What if it drifts ashore? . . . I suppose we could cremate you—"

"It!"

"—It, so it wouldn't be recognized." Sarah paused, frowning. "Unless you think burning it would hurt you. Give you a fever or something. Of course, we already cut it open without you fountaining blood."

At the word "blood," Dante felt his pulse with unnatural distinctness, throbbing in his neck and chest and at the base of his thumb. Goodbye, lovers: Mei's little white teeth and Tania's mound, firm as a peach beneath his hand. Goodbye, Laura my friend: thanks for the pots of green tea we drank in your tiny porcelain cups. Goodbye, Aunt Sophie, with your coins and cigarettes; Sarah with your embroidered vests and acid wit. Goodbye, Mom: with one Scots glance you could size me up to the last pound, shilling, and pence.

Goodbye, Jet: I loved you too well to have done so badly by you.

Ave, Pater: morituri te salutamus.

"We should bury the body," Dante said at last. He glanced at it, slit down the middle, the skin pulled over the sharp ends of the ribs "to avoid puncture wounds during subsequent manipulations."

Jet laid a thin hand on Dante's corpse, touching it on the hip, the groin, gently probing the edges of the slit belly. "I want to know why I'm different." Slowly he stood up, hands leaving the corpse. "I want to know why I wear this," he said, tracing the butterfly birthmark that spread over his cheek.

"So we'll ask Mom and Dad," Dante said. "Sarah can tackle Mom while you and I are burying this . . . thing."

"That's not enough," Jet said softly. "You can't just bury it and walk away, Dante. You're going to die if you don't find out what's going on. And then I'd never find out what happened to me."

"For Christ's sake," Dante said heatedly. "I looked, didn't I? I looked at the damn body; I dragged it down and opened it up—"

("Sort of like a fortune cookie, when you think of it," Sarah murmured.)

"—What the hell else do you want from me?"

Without answering, Jet grabbed Dante's hand and pulled it down onto the corpse's open chest. A surge of dread crackled over Dante's skin as from a prison deep inside himself a forbidden memory broke free, rank with sweat and fear. *The darkness. The heavy chopping of the fan in the next room.*

A huge hand on his leg.

Dante snatched his hand away from the corpse.

"Hey! Boys! Check your testosterone at the door," Sarah said sharply.

Jet shrugged. "An angel is what you are, Dante. You'd better face up to that if you want to stay alive."

"I don't think you know what you're asking of me," Dante murmured.

The butterfly on Jet's cheek trembled. "Everything," he said.

A tiny spider's leg began to clamber up from the body's slit throat. Dante bit his lip until it bled, until the spider crawled away, until he felt the vision seep back inside himself like water soaking into the earth.

"Okay," he said.

CHAPTER
FOUR

EVEN BY THE TIME DANTE AND HIS SIBLINGS WERE
sneaking his dead body out to the boathouse at their
family house a mile outside the City, Laura Chen
was still at work. Long after lights had winked out in the
buildings around her (glass and steel monoliths by I. M.
Pei, with no feeling for the rolling hills or the river—what
had the man been thinking of?), Laura remained behind,
pondering the tricky question of remodeling Mr. Hudson's home. He wanted a solarium, and the logic of his
house suggested that it be built on the southeast corner,
but according to his geomancer the year was not propi-
tious for building in that quadrant.

Sometimes Laura stood hunched and still over the
blueprints spread across her drafting table. Other times

she prowled the office, gulping down cup after cup of strong black coffee as she considered her options.

They could, of course, conduct purifying rituals to attract the influence of the two auspicious stars that Mr. Ling, the geomancer, said were in Hudson's ascendant. Mr. Ling was willing to do his best, but at heart he felt this would be a Band-Aid solution. Laura tended to agree. She had no particular talent for feng shui, though she had a good grasp of its principles, but her architect's sensibilities were enough to convince her that cosmetic quick-fixes were no substitute for building on a solid foundation.

So—if the solarium wasn't to face southeast, where should it go? And how would the rest of the house have to be altered to allow its harmonious integration?

It was at times like these—up late, weary, and struggling with another impossible feng shui problem—that she almost wished her great-uncle had been less famous. It was the exalted name of Chen Dai Fei, one of the Five Founders of the Permitted City, that caused Chinese clients to choose his niece to do their work. Though still only a junior partner at Jaundice & Park, Laura was by far the most at ease working in the interdisciplinary approach the Permitted City project had pioneered. Mr. Jaundice was only really comfortable with engineers and contractors. Ms. Taft had mastered the ergonomists' lingo, and Mr. Park spoke a smattering of sociologese— but only Laura could sit down with a geomancer without feeling silly. Laura always remembered to bury a charm under the foundation stone of a client's house, and she alone in the firm knew how to counteract the inauspicious influence of a hard-lined building going up across the street by the careful placement of a few inexpensive 8-Trigram mirrors.

Not that she believed everything the geomancers told her: divination, though getting better every year, was still an inexact science. Her attitude to the angels she worked with was much like her attitudes about God: clearly there was *something* going on. If she had her doubts from time to time that her priest or geomancer knew exactly what that something was, she still thought it foolish not to say her prayers, or listen to Mr. Ling's advice.

What made this commission particularly delicate was that Mr. Hudson was not Chinese at all, but an eighth-generation American who bled Boston blue. Success in her projects for non-Chinese customers was critical; if these clients prospered, if they felt happy and serene in the houses she designed for them, she would have made her contribution to the work of Tristan Chu, Gary Snyder, and a host of others: convincing Americans that the Permitted City techniques worked. If the American public believed that, her presence would give her firm a decided edge in the marketplace. It had been hinted, even by so august a luminary as old Mr. Jaundice himself, that if the number of wealthy clients seeking her services continued to swell, she might soon find her name appended to the firm's.

Well, Great-uncle's name, she thought wryly. That's what the customers were really paying for.

She poured herself another cup of coffee. Unfortunately, it was not Great-uncle who did the work. (Well—three times Uncle Chen had sent dreams to guide her, but those were exceptions, not the rule, and anyway she preferred to solve her problems on her own.)

It was five cups of coffee past closing time when finally she sighed, rubbed her eyes, and flipped off the lamp over her drafting table. Opening her desk, she reached past her slide rules and mechanical pencils to a thin horsehair brush and a pot of red ink. On special yellow charm paper, thin and crackly as crepe, she inscribed two talismans, one for Chen Dai Fei and one for her father. These she burned in the small grate on her desk, offering up her daily prayer of thanks. Then she belted on her raincoat, locked up, and flipped off the lights.

A paper job, she thought, a little lonely with the lateness of the hour. Drawing paper houses. And my family reduced to paper dolls and shriveled into ash.

Her mother had adamantly refused ever to go back to Kansas. Laura had never even met her cousins there; she talked to her grandparents on the phone twice a year, at Christmas and Easter. They were polite. How could they be more, when they had not been allowed to be part of Laura's family? In some ways she was too Chinese to be American, and yet she had lived all her life under the Stars and Stripes; could still quote the preamble to the Constitution and chant the Pledge of Allegiance, that great charm every American child had to learn. What could China mean to her? She had never been there. Never seen her father in his own country. Never even met the great Dai Fei.

Laura shook her shoulders and gave an angry, horsey snort. She despised self-pity.

Lost Child or Treasure Child, she told herself sternly. Depends on how you look at it. Now stop moping and go to bed!

She looked back at the talismans smoldering in the

grate. A thin advancing emberline gleamed and softly crackled where black ash overwhelmed the yellow paper.

Good night, Uncle Chen.

Good night, Father.

Goodbye.

Perhaps it was the five extra cups of coffee that made her sleep so lightly; that made her snap awake in the middle of the night, and made her left eye tremble. She glanced at her bedside clock: 2:48 A.M.—the hour of Ch'ou. A tic in the left eye foretold . . . What was it again? *Something will happen to worry you.* Or was it *Someone is thinking of you.* Unable to remember, she groped for the 1992 T'ung Shu dangling from its red silk tassel at the head of her bed. She was flipping through the pages of the almanac, trying to remember where the section on Fortune-telling by Physical Sensations was, when she heard a noise from upstairs.

Immediately she knew what must have awakened her. There were footsteps moving around in the apartment overhead. But it wasn't Dante Ratkay: he was spending Thanksgiving weekend at home with his family. Besides, she knew his sleepy tread as he headed for the refrigerator in the middle of the night, or bumped through the darkness to pee. Often enough there were other footsteps overhead—lighter, feminine ones from Dante's traveling circus of lovers—but never footsteps like these: sure, methodical treads that paused, moved a step or two, paused, moved another step . . .

Searching.

Laura sat up in bed, strung tight as a bow. Probably

it was just a thief, she told herself. Just a B&E artist hitting an empty apartment.

On the fourth floor?

It would be an inefficient cat-burglar who couldn't find better pickings closer to the ground. Those footsteps belonged to someone who had chosen Dante's apartment in particular. Probably had even known Dante was away and the coast would be clear.

Or—and this thought scared her—the intruder hadn't known Dante was away; had crept up to his room in the middle of the night, expecting to find him there.

Gently Laura reached for the telephone beside her bed and dialed 911. The clicks as the dial spun back seemed deafening, like machine-gun fire.

Overhead the footsteps suddenly paused.

Laura huddled under her blanket with the phone beneath her. She dragged a pillow over her head to help muffle the sound of her voice.

"Emergency. How can I help you?"

"I think there's an intruder in the apartment above me. The guy who lives there's away—"

"I'm sorry, but I can't hear you. You'll have to speak up."

Laura cringed. "Intruder!" she hissed. "There's an intruder in apartment four-o-six, eighteen eighty-eight Green Street."

"Are you able to get out of the apartment without being seen?"

"I'm not in the apartment, I'm downstairs," Laura grated.

"Then how do you know there's an intruder?"

With enormous restraint Laura kept herself from hurling the phone across the room. Giving up on the cops, she placed the receiver delicately back on its cradle and crept out of bed.

It's ridiculous for me to sneak, she told herself; whoever is up there can't hear my footsteps. But she found herself walking on her toes anyway, calves tight as if she were sparring in her Wenlido class.

She prowled through her apartment, trying to think, winding around the silk panels that separated each area from the next, ducking automatically under the brass lanterns. Either the cops would send someone out or they wouldn't. Even if they did, whoever was upstairs burgling Dante's apartment would be long gone before a patrol car arrived.

They had shared a lot of cups of tea, Dante and Laura; it made her mad to think of someone tearing up his place.

Someone . . . or Something.

She stopped dead. Maybe the thing searching Dante's apartment wasn't human at all. This building wasn't in the slums, but it was only a few blocks from the dreariest part of downtown. If minotaurs had made it as far as Westwood, they could easily be prowling here. And Dante had a bit of angel in him. He tried to ignore it as much as possible, but she had seen him flinch while walking by a mirror. Once, when he wasn't looking, a butterfly had struggled damply from the tea leaves at the bottom of his cup. Laura had said nothing at the time, knowing he wouldn't want to hear about it.

Could Something have been forming in his room? Or had a minotaur wandered in, following the scent of magic up the stairs, tracking its ghostly efflorescence to Dante's door?

Laura stood a long moment in the darkness, six lanky feet of frustration in a plain pink nightgown. She had carried on her father's work, but she never had mastered his easy disposition. Her mother was a big raw-boned woman from a Kansas farming community, and along with her size, Laura had inherited her stubborn temperament. ("Tough as nails"—the phrase had enchanted Laura's father; a wonderfully poetic description of his wife, he thought. Her pet name, Sally Tough-As-Nails, he chanted lovingly in the last soft breath before he died.)

Still fuming over her abortive call to 911, Laura had a sudden inspiration for how she might drive out the intruder, be he minotaur or man. Belting on her silk kimono (the one with the lucky dragon on it—good!), she grabbed a box of wooden matches from a shelf above her refrigerator. From the little cedar votive cabinet beneath the eastern window she grabbed a pack of firecrackers, left over from the New Year, packed together like so many bullets in a paper bandoleer.

Letting herself out of her own apartment, she headed down the corridor for the stairs, striding over the dingy carpet like an angry stork. She was working hard not to think, working just to maintain her anger. She knew that if she faltered, fear would set in. At first she climbed the stairs two at a time, but at the landing caution kicked in and she went more slowly, watching Dante's door and ready to run if a minotaur came out of it, or a man with a gun.

She took the corridor very quietly indeed, stopping a couple of feet from Dante's door, and listening. There: the smooth wooden grumble of a drawer being pulled out.

Laura's heart bumped painfully in her chest.

She suddenly realized how much noise striking her wooden match was going to make. But it was too late to worry about that now. Better get it over with before I sneeze, she thought. Or panic.

Closing her eyes, she mouthed a quick prayer to her ancestors—Uncle Chen, if ever you look out for me, look out for me now!

Quickly she struck a match and held it to the firecracker's fuse. When it caught, she dropped the matches, opened Dante's door a crack, and pitched the firecrackers in. There was a grunt of surprise followed by an instant of total silence. Then the firecrackers went off like gunshots in the darkness.

Inside the apartment someone squawked and crashed heavily to the floor. Tripped over Dante's bedside table, Laura thought, hearing the thump and clang as Dante's telephone and old brass alarm clock clattered to the floor. Whoever was inside swore and scrambled up. Didn't sound like a minotaur, Laura thought. Relief surged through her like whiskey.

Now hold on, she told herself. A normal guy with a normal gun could still fill you full of ordinary holes.

Hesitating outside the door, she heard a shattering crash from inside the apartment.

She inched the door open, and a moment later heard the sound of footsteps clanging on the fire escape. Cursing herself for a coward, she ran inside and fumbled for the dimmers; couldn't find them; lost another few precious seconds until she remembered Dante only had old-fashioned switches for his lights. She cursed again and slapped them on.

A cool breeze eddied from the kitchen, thick with the stink of gunpowder. The window that led out to the fire escape must have been latched. The intruder had smashed it and swept out the glass at the bottom with a wooden cutting board that now lay discarded on the floor. Picking her way to the window in bare feet, Laura just caught a glimpse of a dark figure clattering down the fire escape. "Hey! Stop!" she shouted. Then, "Fire!"— that was supposed to work better.

Her neighbors were not convinced. A couple of them looked curiously out their windows, but no one seemed in the least interested in dashing outside and running down the intruder. He had too much of a start for Laura to have any hope of catching him, and frankly she didn't like the idea of cramming her gangling frame through a window still glittering with broken glass along its top and sides. There was nothing she could do but watch and hope the mysterious intruder would choose to amble under a street light so she could get a nice long look at him.

He didn't.

"Well, damn," Laura said.

She became aware of the way her hands were trembling. In fact, now that she came to think of it, her whole body felt pretty shaky. She decided she should sit on Dante's ghastly white couch for a moment and recover her equilibrium.

"Please," said a distant voice from Dante's bedroom. Adrenaline screamed back into Laura's bloodstream. ". . . Hang up, and try your call again. If you need assistance, dial your operator. Please hang up now. This is a recording."

It was the phone: just the phone.

Laura hissed slowly; tension leaked from her like air from a punctured tire. "Damn," she muttered. She scowled at her big shaking hands. "Must be the coffee," she said.

The cops finally showed up just past four in the morning. Officer Donnelly was young and white and had very pleasant manners, including covering his mouth when he yawned, which he did almost continuously. He had bored a hole through a flattened bullet and strung it on a red ribbon as a walk-away, cinched to a belt-loop at his hip. Officer Pierce was black and middle-aged, too old to believe in walk-aways; he played Grouchy Cop.

The police also brought an angel. "Ugh," she said, walking into Dante's apartment. Laura didn't blame her; she hated Dante's apartment too, calculated as it was to be as flatly impersonal as possible. The angel grimaced, looking around at the white-painted bookshelves, the white-painted table and plain painted chairs. Everything bought new, of course: Dante avoided antique and design stores as if they were leper colonies.

The angel squinted unhappily. "What's wrong with the light?"

"He buys old-fashioned incandescents and there's no dimmer."

The angel peered disbelievingly at the (plain white) lamp beside Dante's coffee table. "They're not even full-spectrum bulbs?"

Laura laughed, remembering that she had said pretty much the same thing in pretty much the same tone of voice three years ago when Dante had first invited her to drop by. Personally, she used Morning bulbs over her breakfast table and had a three-track dimmer to keep her living room light levels harmoniously adjusted. "Awful, isn't it?"

"Yuck," the angel agreed. She was a thin-faced woman in her early thirties who wore three charms on a red cord around her neck: a large irregular pearl overwritten with tiny Chinese characters, a pierced metal cap from a bottle of Coke, and mounted on a gold ring a fragment of what looked to be glass from a shattered windshield—presumably a walk-away from some accident. She had a four-character chop tattooed on her face: "Pearl," "River," and one Laura read as "Traveling," all around a Phoenix. She had a habit of periodically hunching her shoulders and peering out from between them, a mannerism which made her look like a questing ferret. It was particularly pronounced when she was running her fingers over Dante's dresser drawers, and around the frame of the smashed window. Every time she did it, Officer Pierce would shoot a questioning look at her, accompanied by an impatient grunt.

At first the angel volunteered her information quickly enough: one intruder; male; looking for something. Had been alarmed while in the bedroom.

"Extraordinary," Officer Pierce growled, looking down at the blackened package of firecrackers still lying on Dante's (bare, painted) living-room floor. "What would we do without you?"

"A question I often ask myself," the angel shot back.

Pierce rolled his eyes.

While the young white cop took Laura's statement, Pierce strolled around the apartment, listening and making notes. As far as Laura could tell, nothing had been stolen.

The angel's shoulders jerked as she bent over Dante's dresser. A curious, guarded expression came over her face.

"Well?"

The angel glanced back at Pierce. "Nothing . . . definite," she said.

He scowled.

Brushing her skirt away from her knees, the angel knelt down and ran her fingertips over the handle of one of the drawers, very, very carefully, as if stroking a venomous snake. Her shoulders jumped up and she hissed with a sharp intake of breath.

Pierce's scowl deepened. "What have you got?"

"Not—not much," the angel stammered. Unthinkingly, she reached to touch the pearl hanging from her neck.

"It's some angel thing, isn't it? You all get that shifty look when you're concealing evidence."

The angel stood up, bristling. "I get paid by the hour, Sergeant, whether I'm here or at my desk. I'm perfectly happy to let you handle this on your own, if that's what you want."

"Now, now," young Donnelly said soothingly. "We all know it's late and tempers are a little—Awhh! (yawn!) Excuse me!—are a little short. Let's try to get along." He held up his hands diplomatically. He was smart enough not to direct his charm at Officer Pierce, Laura noticed.

Pierce rolled his eyes. He did it with an expressive power and economy of movement that suggested frequent practice. Scowling, he turned back to Laura. "You know the occupant?" Laura nodded. "What's he do?"

"He works in a biology lab at the University."

"Student?"

"No. Just a paid tech. Dropped out halfway through his Master's."

"How long has he been living here?"

"Three years, I think. He was here when I moved in."

Officer Pierce's eyebrows rose in some surprise. He looked around the room. "Awfully bare for a place someone's been living for three years. No television, no record player, no magazines. Everything neat."

Laura shrugged. "He spends a lot of time out. If Dante wants to watch something, he goes to the movies. If he wants music, he goes to a club, or the symphony. He always preferred the place bare. Less to clean up if you bring home, um, company, he says."

"Company?"

They heard the angel laugh sharply from the kitchen. "A stack of condoms in his bedroom drawer," she explained. "No bread or milk in the fridge, but a tin of pâté and two bottles of wine. Ooh, very nice," she added. "Front-du-Lac '84."

Officer Donnelly grinned broadly, and a small smile even escaped Officer Pierce. "Did Mr.—"

"Ratkay."

"—Ratkay have any enemies you know of, Ms. Chen?" He glanced at the bedroom. "Disappointed girl-friends, for instance?"

After a moment, Laura shook her head. "I don't think so. He was never really close with any of them. Dante's a nice guy, but he doesn't have the guts to get serious."

Officer Pierce studied his notepad. "Not even with you?"

Laura laughed. "I'm not stupid, Sergeant. We're good friends, that's all. He drops by my apartment two or three times a week and we drink tea."

"Funny. Sounds like the kind of guy who would have made a pass."

"You think I would have accepted?" Laura said lightly, but something about Pierce's comment needled her. Come to think of it, why *hadn't* Dante ever given her a line? She was no beauty, but then most of his women weren't. She wouldn't have taken him up on it, but it was galling to think she didn't live up to even Dante's fairly catholic standards.

Laura knew she wanted a husband and a family—just not quite yet. Was there something in her manner that warned men off? If so, she'd better find out what it was before she started looking for a mate; any signals that put off Dante Ratkay must be pretty hard to ignore.

Or—and this was another disturbing thought—maybe he had made a pass at her and she hadn't even noticed it. Was work absorbing so much of her attention (along with taking care of Mother), that the rest of life was passing her by?

A quick surge of loneliness washed through Laura. She found herself wishing that Dante were here himself, smartly dressed even in the wee hours and making coffee in the little espresso machine, answering questions with his indefatigable charm, joking with her and admiring (as he would) her courage in having driven the Bad Guy off.

But of course he was at the family home she envied so much, sleeping soundly in his childhood bed, no doubt, with the river rolling on at the bottom of the garden. He had a place to go home to for Thanksgiving, where he could still be someone's brother, someone's child. Unlike Laura, who never had a brother or a sister. Who was the only grown-up in her family now.

And what a grown-up thing to do: sit here feeling sorry for yourself! Laura thought, tartly reprimanding herself. *It's the hour that's making you gloomy, and the after-shock from the excitement.*

A faint, acrid smell of gunpowder still lingered in the living room, though a cold draft crept in from the broken kitchen window.

Officer Donnelly's hand crept to his mouth, and Laura couldn't help yawning herself.

"Almost done, Ms. Chen. Can you tell us what the firecrackers were all about?"

"To scare off evil spirits," the angel in the kitchen said promptly. "Right?"

Laura nodded. "I read about the Westwood minotaur in the paper yesterday. Dante has a bit of angel in him, so I guess it was on my mind."

"Does it work?" Donnelly asked, squatting down to examine the pack of used firecrackers with renewed interest.

Laura shrugged. "I don't know. It's what they do in China, and they never forgot how to deal with their ghosts and angels there. That's what my dad used to say, anyway."

Officer Donnelly smiled and touched the walk-away clipped to his belt. "Man, anything to help out if we run into one of those creepy things."

"I think you'll find a clip of firecrackers in your holster

there, Mr. Donnelly," Officer Pierce said witheringly. "A neat little firework that shoots off a steel-jacketed rocket, in fact." He looked back at his notebook. "Hey," he called into the kitchen, glowering. "Why didn't you tell me the occupant was an angel?"

The police angel returned. In her left hand she held a butcher knife, taken from the block on Dante's kitchen counter. "I don't know," she said slowly. "There's something . . . odd." She tapped the knife blade absently with her fingernails, and her shoulders hunched as she glanced at Laura. "Is your friend scheduled to go into the hospital? Elective surgery, something like that?"

"Not that I know of," Laura said, mystified.

"Oh." The angel's shoulders jumped again. With a small shudder of distaste, she slid the knife carefully back into its block. "Do you have the number where he's staying?"

"That's enough," Officer Pierce growled. "We'll be contacting Mr. Ratkay in the morning. Ms. Chen, if you speak to him before we do, please have him come down to the station and make a report. We'd like him to confirm that nothing's been stolen."

"What do you mean?" Laura demanded, glaring at the angel and now thoroughly alarmed. "You think I should call him?"

"No. Well—no." Briskly, the angel shrugged. "Might as well wait until morning. I don't think calling would matter much . . . one way or the other," she added, half to herself. "But if I were him, I'd see a doctor soon. And watch out for butter—"

She stopped herself with a quick jerk of her shoulders. Her eyes narrowed.

"Watch out for butter?" Laura repeated, confused. "You mean his heart? He comes from this Hungarian family; they eat about a cow a week. They spread lard on toast. I keep telling him it's slow suicide."

The angel blinked and smiled. "Sorry. I shouldn't have said anything. I think my own wires are crossed, is what it is." She yawned elaborately, avoiding Officer Pierce's suspicious gaze. She glanced meaningfully at young Donnelly. "Sure is a long night, isn't it?"

It sure is, Laura thought, as the cops slowly got ready to leave. When they were gone she swept up the smashed glass in the kitchen and covered the broken window in plastic wrap.

A long night.

But tired as she was, she couldn't sleep when she went back to bed. She lay there with her eyes stubbornly closed for almost an hour before admitting defeat. Finally with a resentful groan she heaved herself up, rummaged through her desk for a brush, ink, and three sheets of yellow charm paper like the stuff she kept at work. On them she drew three of Heavenly Master Chang's best charms. Going up to Dante's apartment, she taped the first charm, to protect the home, over the broken window. The second, a charm to prevent the entry of wild animals, she taped over his door. Finally she hid the Hundred Different Things Charm behind the headboard of his bed, where he wouldn't see it and take it down.

Feeling silly and determined all at once, she faced east, looking out the broken kitchen window at the murky maze of tenements and street lamps, and recited in her rusty Mandarin the incantation her father had taught her to lend power to Chang Tien-shih's charms:

"The universe and yin-yang are wide, the sun comes out from the east. I use this charm to get rid of all evils. My mouth spits outs strong fire, my eyes can shine out rays like the sun. I can ask the Heavenly Soldiers to catch the devils and get all sickness out of the house. Heavenly soldiers can suppress evils and create luck. Let the Law be obeyed; let this order be executed straightaway."

Taking a sip of water from Dante's tap, she bowed to the east, clenched her teeth three times, and spat it out.

Then and only then, at ease at last and thoroughly exhausted, she clumped back downstairs and fell heavily into bed, and sleep.

NOW HE GOES ALONG THE DARK ROAD, WHENCE THEY
SAY NO ONE RETURNS.   —CATULLUS

CHAPTER
FIVE

PORTRAIT
I prefer to shoot in black and white.

*Usually, when you say of a man, "He sees things
in black and white" you mean he is inflexible and dog-
matic; he treats complex issues with brutal simplicity. In
fact, you should mean just the opposite. It is color film
that embalms its subjects in workaday reality. Black and
white leaves room for mystery, for subtle shades of gray.
Without hue, the eye becomes aware of complexities of
shadow and texture; you haven't really seen the texture
of grass or sand or sea until you've studied one of An-
derson's black and white studies of the Atlantic off the
empty New England coast.*

This, now: this is a portrait of Dante, black and white,

that I took of him with my old Kodak the summer we were fifteen. We had just finished building the tree-fort in the big willow on Three Hawk Island. We built it airily, in the Chinese style, with a strong rail waist-high all the way around, and the rest of the walls made of bamboo blinds. When the wind blew, they clicked and rustled, murmuring in long, slow conversation with the twisting willow leaves, the running river.

It took six weeks to build that fort, six weeks of building through the long summer afternoons while the sun tanned the willow green, listening to the sap well and beat beneath its bark.

Six weeks of feeling the willow's long, slow grief.

Dante tried to ignore it, but even I could tell it was a tree that had known too much remorse. Even at summer's heart, its leaves never lost a certain gray pallor. Even on the calmest day, a sad breeze sighed through its trailing fronds. The river had eaten away at the island's southern tip, exposing the willow's great black roots, and I used to find myself wondering what lay trapped in the shadows beneath the river's surface there. What did the black roots pierce, and piercing, draw into themselves?

Then too there were the scars on its trunk and on many a broad limb where strips of bark two fingers wide and a handspan long had been carefully peeled away, seventy or eighty of them. Never clustered too closely together, never anything that might ring the tree or kill one of its boughs. Sap gummed these wounds like scabbing blood.

At first I thought those welts must be the cause of the willow's restless grief, but Dante told me once the opposite was true. He didn't know the story, he said; didn't want to. But he knew something lingered, some tincture of remorse for events now unremembered, that made gifts of these scars; each one a chance for penance. (For long after guilty memories fade, the urge for penance lingers: strong and blind as the will to drink rain and grope for sunlight.)

Maybe in the end it was the willow's melancholy that drove him away. Dante was never one to suffer clouds in his endless sky.

In this picture Dante is perched on the fort's west rail, one leg stretched out, the other dangling down. It is late afternoon. The sunlight is low, coming right down the river valley; it burns like silver along the line of his leg. Willow shadows knot and tangle on the bamboo walls.

In life what you notice about Dante is the curly red-gold hair, the pale complexion, the freckles, the smile. But here in black and white you see the restlessness in his limbs, the hunch of his shoulders and the line of a flaring eyebrow as he squints upstream into a dazzle of sun. We had just spent weeks building this fort; poured countless hours into planning and constructing it, argued every detail of materials and tools and cost, ridden into the City on the bus and plunged into Chinatown looking for blinds and red lacquer and a set of glass chimes in the shape of dragonflies. But looking at the picture, you can tell Dante is already leaving this place, putting it behind him, gazing restlessly into the future, as if like Lot or Orpheus the world would be lost if he dared look back.

Dante—gregarious, charming, facile—thinks we could hardly be more different: day and night, sun and moon. He's wrong, of course: we just carry our aloneness dif-

ferently. Mine is no secret. I stand always apart from the center of things, observing. Dante, on the other hand, carries his isolation into every crowd. He laughs and jokes and seizes conversation, satanic eyebrows flaring . . . but he only lends himself: he never gives. He never stays, he never puts down roots. He floats through time, too cagey to dock or let an anchor down; and life drifts by him on the bank.

It is a picture I return to: the two of us, in the place we built together. Dante, already eager to be gone; and me, behind the camera, absent from the picture, as if I wasn't even there.

It was the dark gray before dawn, clammy and cold, as Dante and Jet lowered the boat into the river with the corpse propped awkwardly across the thwarts. Jet sat in the stern, his pale hand resting on the tiller of the little Evinrude engine, just above the cadaver's head. Dante sat in the prow. When the boat rocked, his own dead feet bumped against his thigh. Rigor mortis had started, stiffening the corpse's face and neck. According to Dr. Ratkay's autopsy book, rigor would proceed down the length of the body from head to toe, passing off in the same order twenty-four to forty-eight hours later.

A chilly fog hung over the river. Billows moved heavily through it, following and overspreading one another. The damp cold ate into Dante like rigor mortis, bringing slow paralysis into his face and fingers, and his breath steamed up into the blinding fog that hemmed them in, making of their boat a little rocking world with only three inhabitants, two living and one dead. The only sounds were the chugging of the old Evinrude and the slap of the river against the bow. Once Dante peered back through the gloom, his eyes drawn to his corpse, only to see its chest and head thickly wreathed in mist, as if it were a candle guttering into clouds of cold gray smoke. With one hand on the tiller, Jet sat beside it, implacable as Charon.

Dante hunched down against the cold and blew into his hands to warm them. He did not look back again.

Some time later Jet said, "I see the willow." He flipped the engine into reverse to slow them down.

A cloud of fog passed, and Dante, caught off guard, saw the great willow on Three Hawk Island with angel's eyes. Suddenly it loomed over him, showing itself with the force of a secret revealed: its trunk a great heart, splitting into ventricles, each bough an artery, each branch a vein, twigs tangled and dwindling into hair-thin capillaries; vessels and veins plucked whole from a giant's body and revealed to him, like the maps of the human circulatory system his father had tried to make him look at in the fearful pages of Gray's *Anatomy*.

If one were a fish—a pike, say—what might one find in the hollow pool at the willow's base?

What grief or guilt had lain there all these years, trapped, decaying, bleeding into the water the willow drank, the soil it consumed?

Jet nosed the boat around the point of Three Hawk Island and into a shallow bay on the southern side. It was a good spot to bury a body. Here they had moorage for the boat and would be shielded from the eyes of anyone on the north shore, including their parents. The river's south bank, steep and shadowy and cold, was almost uninhabited.

Dante jumped onto the island and pulled the boat up on shore. Slowly he walked to the base of the big willow, squinting up into the branches. "Is the fort still there?"

"Yes."

A little puff of wind roiled through a cloud of fog; from the shadows overhead came a low, ghostly groan, and a hollow clacking, like the bones of a hanged man stirring in the breeze. Wind chimes, Dante realized with a start. Jet must have replaced the original glass chimes with bamboo ones that held a deeper, more haunting and melancholy music.

"I fixed it up myself a few weeks ago," Jet continued. "A new coat of lacquer on the roof, another can of Thompson's on the rest." Jet grinned at Dante's look of surprise. "I still come here, you know. I sweep it out every autumn, after the willow drops its leaves. If you'd been paying attention, you would have seen the blinds rolled up and stashed in the boathouse."

"I guess I had other things on my mind."

"Not to mention your liver." Jet joined him at the willow's foot, leaning his back against the hoary bole. "We used to have a hell of a time keeping Sarah out of here."

Dante grinned, remembering. "We beat back the Powells and Hewletts and the Baggy boys, but Sarah was a whole other situation."

"We were handicapped," Jet pointed out. "We couldn't use slingshots."

"Ah. Right you are."

Overhead the sky was paling. A soft plop carried from the south bank, as of something slipping into the river. A mink, Dante thought. Or possibly a marten.

They stood together in the gray morning, looking

south. From time to time an eddy in the fog would reveal the far bank. Jet's eyes, for once empty of calculation or cold amusement, were unreadable, fixed on the darkness of the far shore. "The fort was ours," he said finally. "Yours and mine. Everyone else was a stranger." Naked willow-fronds hung around them, dripping cold tears of dew.

Dante reached up to the willow's trunk and touched a welt, chest-high, where someone had stripped off a ribbon of bark. Aunt Sophie, he realized. Aunt Sophie complaining of her rheumatism, sipping her cup of bitter willow-bark tea. Jet would have known that, of course; would have watched, hidden in the fort, as she took her slices of bark. He was still the little spy she had found in her bassinet, a baby no longer wholly her child, with a mark of Cain newly etched on his face.

Dante sighed. He had a lot to do in seven days. He squinted up at the brightening sky and corrected himself: six and a half.

Dante shuddered as a fragment of dream came back to him: the magic lure glimmering and winking, leading him down into strange depths of sleep. The night before last, he thought wearily. The last time he had slept, before he had crept out into another gray dawn and tried his luck fishing with a wasp-bodied lure.

They decided to bury the body in the shallow depression under a fallen tree, now rotten and cancered with moss. They dug quickly. Made from silt and leaf mold and years of mud, the dirt here was startlingly black, moist and rich as chocolate cake.

"How long had you known?" Dante asked. Before setting off in the boat he had returned to the house to swap his silk jacket for a leather one decorated with Braque stencils. Now he stripped it off as sweat began to bead like dew on his high forehead.

"Known?"

Dante glanced back at the boat, where his patient body waited.

"Ah," Jet said. He bent back to his task. "Not long."

"But you checked under the blanket. In my room." Reluctantly, Jet nodded. "Other people always called you sneaky," Dante said. He drove his shovel down. "I told them they were wrong. I told them you wouldn't pry where you didn't belong."

"I don't *belong* anywhere—had you forgotten? I live at the edge of the known world, gnawing the bones you throw me from the table."

"Spare me your self-pity."

Jet stopped, his fingers tight around the haft of his shovel. "You were too scared to look, Dante. Somebody had to." Jet bent back to work. "I didn't think to check under the blanket for a long time," he said softly. "I may be cursed, but I ain't no angel. . . . I didn't feel anything growing under the blanket. It was years before I realized you were afraid of it."

Jet squinted, as if trying to see into the past. "You had been visiting, but you were about to go back to the City for a date. Amalia Jensen, I believe it was." (Here Dante, remembering, would have blushed had his face not already been red with exertion. He grunted and flung another shovelful of dirt into the bushes.) "You were preening and ignoring me while I warned you about her and that loathsome Todd fellow. You ran the comb through your hair and without thinking reached for the blanket—so you could look at yourself in the mirror, I suppose. When you touched it, I could see the shock go through you, as if you'd stuck your finger in a socket. You turned pale as a ghost, babbled some excuse, and bolted into the bathroom."

Dante shook his head. "I don't remember any of this."

"I'm not surprised," Jet said dryly. "I'm sure you did your usual sterling job of forgetting any unpleasantness. You do remember what happened with Amalia, don't you?"

"Shut up."

Jet snickered. "After that, I would make faces in the mirror every now and then, and check under the blanket, to see what sprouted there. For a long time nothing did, and I was worried."

Dante snorted. "Bored, you mean."

"Well, seriously, Dante: you are my only real enter-tainment, you know. So finally on one of your visits home—Christmas two years ago—I decided to tiptoe into your room while you were sleeping. Things were different with you there. Instead of feeling the usual jum-ble when I ran my hand over the blanket, there was something long and smooth and solid. But that was the last time you slept in your room until this visit. You al-ways came up with some excuse to drive back to the City, or crash on the parlor sofa."

"I only felt safe if I could hear Grandfather Clock," Dante admitted.

They worked in silence for a long time. The heavy chopping of the spades, his and Jet's, beat unevenly like the blades of a windshield wiper, like their two hammers pounding nails into the fort in the old willow. Memories rushed over Dante like clouds: the thin fierce darkness of Jet's body, stooping next to his, digging in the dirt of some sandbox, his lank hair falling over his eyes, scowling with concentration. Jet wrapped around a tree limb, hammering up from underneath at an awkward nail while the scent of willow-sap bled into the summer air around them. Shadows rushed over Dante; all those times he had felt Jet's loneliness, Jet hammering it at him like a nail, like the steel blade of a shovel chopping into soft earth.

And Dante had always fled that steel touch because he couldn't bear the enormity of Jet's loneliness. He was powerless to fix it. Even to acknowledge it was to feel the chained angel stirring in himself, brooding beneath bright wings on its terrible thoughts of guilt and dread. Stuttering Ann-Marie Bissell, with her bruised cheeks and her mustard sandwiches for lunch. The touch of a huge hand on Duane's leg. The glassy clink at the bottom of Mrs. Farrell's desk; her cloudy eyes when the children filed back into class after lunch.

He dug, and watched himself digging in Jet, as if seeing his reflection in a dark mirror. The chop of the shovel, biting down, the twist of the haft in his hands, the sudden weight on his trembling biceps, his back aching as he turned and dumped the dirt beside the grave.

I'm dying, Dante thought. I'm dying, and my life is passing before my angel eyes. And with each chop of the shovel, a wind blew through him, as if from the beating of great wings, and he was dizzy with the nearness of death.

They stopped at the same moment, panting, slumped over their shovels. The pit was six feet long and almost three feet deep, with narrow, sloping sides. Jet grunted and crisply drove in his spade, shaping the walls. "We want these nice and straight."

"Don't worry," Dante drawled. "You'll get another chance to practice." He chopped down with his shovel, squaring off the head of the grave and accidentally cutting through an earthworm. The worm's front half writhed in the fill dirt. The severed back end twitched and knotted for a long moment, hanging from the grave wall, and then fell in.

A flush of nausea spread out from Dante's stomach, where the growth was, making his limbs watery. Blood pounded in his head.

"Are you all right?"

"No." Dante stood back from his grave. "I think we're about done, don't you?"

The dawn had come, but dully, through a sky leaded with clouds. Ghosts of fog still drifted forlornly over the water, seeking shelter in the dark hollows of the south bank.

Dante watched the worm-half writhe and twine at the bottom of his grave.

Jet said, "I guess we better put him in."

They went back to the rowboat and lifted the body out. Jet took its arms and head; Dante took its feet.

"By last Christmas I knew," Jet grunted, shuffling backwards, his hands hooked under the cadaver's armpits. Its white hands dragged through crumbled bits of fern and last year's leaves. "The shape under the blanket was unmistakable, if you were looking for it."

Together they ducked under the fallen tree and lowered Dante's corpse into its miserable grave. It looked thin and white and terribly fragile, huddled there; defenseless as an unborn child. Jet scooped up a handful of earth and let it sift down onto the body. "Ashes to ashes, dust to dirt. As it was in the beginning, so it shall be in the end. *In nomine Patris, Filii, et Spiritus Sancti.*"

They stood together for a moment, looking down. "It was as if you had died," Jet said softly. "And I was thinking, They won't ask me to say the eulogy." He shook his head. "And that drove me crazy. . . . Why, Dante? Why won't they let me say the words? Why aren't we brothers?" Jet glanced at Dante. "I've never been family. And you know, until I saw your body under the blanket I would have said it didn't matter. I would have said I couldn't miss what I never had."

(But you did miss it, Dante thought. He remembered Jet's cold eyes, black and hard as pebbles, watching him walk out onto the cracking ice; remembered the hunger flickering there. I felt it every hour of every day, he thought. I felt you on me like a leech.)

"But I would have been wrong." Jet paused, squatting at the head of the grave, looking off into a distance measured in years. "Why, Dante? Why should I have to crawl around the corners of my own house like a cockroach at the baseboards? I've never been family and that's been everything. That's been the whole arc and trajectory of my life."

"You're such a whiner," Dante said angrily. "I didn't kick you into any corners."

"Why am I always taking pictures of your life? Why shouldn't I have a life of my own?"

The old familiar rage was pounding in Dante: the tight,

twisting anger only Jet could provoke. "Well you can't have mine!"

"Why not?" Jet said coolly. "You're almost done with it."

Dante leapt for him but Jet twisted and he missed, off balance. Quick as a snake, Jet grabbed his arms and shoved. Dante fell back with Jet on top of him. Something gouged his back and he yelled in pain. He tried to roll away but there was no room to move. Jet drove his face into a wall of black dirt.

He was trapped in his own narrow grave.

The angel ran loose inside Dante, tasting the dirt and the stink of death, the prick of splintered ribs beneath his back. He felt Jet's white fingers wrapping like roots around his wrists to suck the life out of him. Black dirt smeared Dante's hair and face and filled his nose, its moldy muddiness thick in his mouth. Gasping and choking he heaved, pinned under Jet, crushed into his own grave, feeling his own dead body, its skin split and gaping underneath him. "Daddy!" he screamed.

And then Jet rolled off Dante, like a boulder rolling from the mouth of a cave, letting in a rush of gray daylight.

Still screaming, Dante struggled out of his grave and lunged away on all fours, blind with panic, scrabbling until he ran into a tree trunk and dropped like a stone, stunned.

He breathed. His chest heaved, great shuddering gasps, facedown in the leaf mold. At last he rolled over onto his back and lay there, looking up into the cloudy sky through the bare branches of a young willow tree.

Beneath him the ground was cold and damp. His head ached. For a long time he lay panting, resting his eyes on the soft sky; watching its subtle, rolling formlessness. The willow-wands were no longer arteries and veins: daylight had broken their enchantment, left them stiff and woody. Ordinary.

Jet put his hand on Dante's shoulder. "Hey."

Dante grabbed it, fiercely, as if it were an oar coming to him over cracking ice. "I don't want to die," he whispered.

Jet's fingers tightened on his shoulder.

"I don't want to die."

Jet held his hand. "Lo, you have come through the valley of the shadow," he murmured. His hand was warm and thin and strong. "It's okay, D. It's okay."

In plain gray daylight the river was just the river again, muddy-brown and quick with spring run-off. On its banks were only trees and ferns; the sunrise had destroyed its ghosts and spirits. Far down the river valley, Dante could see the usual film of smog hovering over the City. He could hear the traffic on the highway a half-mile behind their house; the clank and roar of a diesel truck booming along, the beeping of an irate commuter.

Dante took a deep breath. The angel in him closed its eyes, and folded its bright wings.

"Well, it's morning," he said.

CHAPTER
SIX

PORTRAIT
   This is a picture of Sarah and Mother together. Mother is sitting at the kitchen table with a cup of coffee; Sarah has been drawing with crayons. Sarah is eight years old. Grandmother and Aunt Sophie have already lavished great Magyar hordes of Hungarian-ness on her: she is dressed in a beautiful little frock, coarsely embroidered in the Hungarian style with tangles of fist-sized poppies and roses. She wears the frock in utter ignorance, like a linebacker. A ponytail spills down her thin back as she leans towards Mother with her tummy on the table, obscuring her drawing. She is lecturing Mother on some Important Issue, such as the necessity of being nice to our animal friends. Mother's eyes are

grave and attentive; she hides a smile behind her coffee cup.

Mother always liked Sarah best. Of course, she loved them both, but she was most comfortable with Sarah. Dante . . . I don't think Mother ever recovered enough from what happened to me to be completely at ease with my twin. There was always a wariness in her eyes, watching him. Waiting for him to vanish into the same darkness that had swallowed Sophie's child.

—Or maybe she just always wanted a girl.

For *whatever* reason, Sarah and Mother are very close. You can see it in the picture: in Sarah's fearlessness, and Mother's hidden smile.

This is from a time when Mother's fiery hair had not yet turned gray; the skin on her hands, smooth and tight, had not yet begun to wrinkle and hang around her joints. In that time it was summer and she wore a flowered skirt and a short-sleeved cotton blouse. Now her blouses all have long sleeves and she always wears a silk kerchief around her neck. More comfortable than jewelry, she says.

This picture of Sarah is from long before that glowering scrap of a kid would grow into a chubby, sullen teenager, before she would run off with a creep and exchange her adolescent's insecurities for an adult shame, a secret she carried in herself like a stone.

It is important to have a sense of humor if you take a lot of photographs. If one were unable to appreciate the subtle ironies of time, the gifts it gives your subjects, and the ones it strips relentlessly away . . .

As the years go by, every picture steeps in the remembrance of false hopes, brief passions, desires and disap-

*pointments. If you didn't have a sense of humor,
photographs would be unbearably tragic.*

Almost any photograph. This one, here.

My little sister Sarah.

*Maybe Fate singled out Aunt Sophie less than she
thought. Maybe, to a parent, every child is a child lost.
In time.*

As Dante and Jet finished burying the body, Sarah was
in the kitchen, trying her new act out on her mother.
Above all things, Gwen Ratkay loved a good joke. The
plan was to get her involved in constructing the routine;
then, at an opportune moment, Sarah would sidle around
to asking about Aunt Sophie's Past.

It wasn't much of a plan, Sarah conceded, but impro-
visation was her life.

Her mother sat at the battle-scarred kitchen table
drinking coffee from the mug Sarah had given her last
Christmas, an ink-black lacquered beauty with one simple design, a branch from a cherry tree, breaking into
pale pink blossom. It was barely seven on a Saturday
morning, but Gwen was already neatly turned out in a
sensible blue skirt and plain white blouse. A kerchief of
Thai silk, dyed turquoise-blue and jade-green, livened up
her sober outfit, as laughter brought the life into her
steady, practical face.

What Sarah loved most about her mother was that she
laughed; freely and superbly from her own steady confidence. Sarah worshipped that. Her own laughter seemed
to her so angry, so fearful and insecure, like the yap of
a hyena. Sarah had a favorite piece of jewelry, a cameo

her grandmother had given her a month before she died. It was very simple, an elegant woman's profile on a plain black background. Sarah wore it as a charm. She knew her father would disapprove if he knew, but she needed it; she wanted so desperately to call up such a woman from inside herself: poised and superb, graceful and witty and kind.

"—So, magic: what a concept, hunh? Can you imagine what the world would be like if magic hadn't started running back into it after World War Two? Ever stop to think about it?" Sarah asked, goggling out at an imaginary crowd.

Mother's lip trembled. With Sarah's round face wavering and her small mouth working, she looked uncommonly like a tuna trying to do calculus.

"I mean, take *Star Wars*. Without the Jungian explosion, it doesn't even get made, right? Let alone win an Oscar. I mean, think about it: without all that archetypal confronting-the-darkness-and-feeling-the-magic stuff, what we have here is basically *Gidget Goes to the Death Star*. Can you imagine anyone financing this in, say, a Freudian world? I mean, you'd have to throw in all kinds of stuff about Luke trying to kill his own father and marry his sister and . . . stuff."

Sarah paused, round face becoming thoughtful. "Okay—bad example. But, um . . . What if we were all Marxists, God help us? Then your blockbuster classic would have to be about a small group of comrades banding together to bring down the Imperialist . . ." The same slow frown settled on her face. ". . . the Imperialist overlords."

Sarah goggled again, and was rewarded with a chuckle

from her audience. Mother sipped from her coffee, grinning.

Sarah held up her hands defensively. "Okay! Okay, but still . . . Personal Development. That's what magic was going to be about, you know. Personal Development. Gonna free up a lot of repressed psychic energies. The McCarthy hearings were the last attempt to deny magic, and when they collapsed, we would all have to face our own internal enigmas:

> "Two, four, six, eight:
> Time to individuate!
> Ego! Psyche! An-i-mus!"

Pause. "Welcome to the end of the Millennium, folks." Sarah held up a page of her script. "I hold in my hand a survey done by Dr. Milton Chesterfield—no, really!— eminent sociologist at Purdue University. And do you know what Dr. Chesterfield's research has revealed? The best-paid profession for angels, the one with the greatest upward mobility is—prostitution!

"Prostitution! Apparently it's all the rage in expensive circles to hire a companion who *really* knows what you want." The puzzled frown settled over Sarah's features again. One eyebrow crept slowly upwards in dawning alarm. ". . . Frankly, I find this hard to believe. I don't know about the rest of you girls, but when I'm having sex, the last thing I want is for him to know what's on my mind."

Mother chortled in mid-sip, blowing inadvertent bubbles in her coffee.

"I mean, how many passionate moments can survive

a sudden, 'But I don't have a beard. And who the hell is Raoul?'

"Not to mention, fellows, that whether you're *really* a fabulous lover is something only your girlfriend and her twenty closest intimates know for sure. You do *not* want the truth here, trust me."

Sarah rolled her eyes and shook her head chidingly at her imaginary audience. "My brother actually had the nerve to ask me once why women fake orgasm. Can you imagine? What a stupid question! Come on, girls: Why do women fake orgasm?" Nodding. "Because men fake foreplay! . . . What a stupid question."

Mother choked on her coffee, snorting with laughter, then glanced guiltily toward the parlor, where Father sat reading the morning paper.

Sarah grinned. "Okay! Okay, so my brother doesn't like this answer. He's a Ladies' Man. Seriously, he's a beacon of hope to women everywhere: a funny, intelligent guy who will have sex with any woman over sixteen—thin, fat, incontinent or insane."

(Oops. Sarah gulped. Oh, well: Mother probably knew all this stuff already.)

"Seriously, my brother loves women's bodies. Almost any woman's body. Now, this is not a family trait. Personally, I hate my body so much, it's started to hate me back." Sarah stuttered for a moment, stricken by her mother's frown. Ashamed. Ashamed and angry, she thought savagely. How well she knew that particular combination. "Anyway, my brother is more forgiving. Like a lawnmower is forgiving, you know? Anything in its path . . .

"He has the best pickup line in the universe. Seriously.

He ambles up to the object of his desires—we'll call her 'the kill'—makes eye contact in a lazy, playful, balding kind of way, and says, 'Make a pass at me.' "

Sarah closed her eyes and sucked the air between her teeth. "Lethal, hunh?"

Mother laughed, but a look that Sarah knew well glinted in her eyes, as if she were studying an unsatisfactory report card. "Does he really say that?"

"Oh yes."

"Does it work?"

Sarah nodded solemnly.

Mother shivered. "I feel like Frankenstein."

"That explains why I so often feel like Igor." Sarah resumed her stage stance. "Seriously, though, my brother is an angel himself— No, really. He says it's not like what people think at all. No mind-reading or anything."

Sarah paused. "This I am prepared to believe. All night long he's dreaming about roulette: 'Thirty-one black! Thirty-one black!' he dreams.

"The next day he drags me off to the casino. 'Sis,' he says, 'I got a sure thing on thirty-one black. I had this dream where I felt this intense, tingling, numb sort of feeling, and the ball kept rolling onto thirty-one black. It's a dead cinch.'

" 'Oh yeah?' I say. 'What's that got to do with me?'

"He wets his lips. 'Uh, I dreamt you gave me a hundred bucks to make the bet,' he says.

"And what the hell, he was right: everything came out like he predicted. We went in, put down the hundred dollars, lost it, and then, while we were standing there in numbed, tingling shock watching my rent go down the tubes, Whammo! The very next spin the wheel comes up thirty-one black. . . .

"Seriously, can you believe the money the Pentagon used to put into angel research? I mean, talk about a waste of tax dollars. Angels don't even blow up when you drop 'em out a plane—they just hit with a wet thud. I pushed my brother out of a tree once: I know."

Oops. "Just a joke," Sarah gulped.

Her mother eyed her narrowly. "Un-hunh."

Sarah swallowed. Improvising, she reminded herself, was her life. "So they spend about seven point four jillion dollars trying to use angels to predict the movements of enemy submarines and shit. What do they get?" Intoning spookily: " 'My mother's cat, screaming at the heart of midnight, and a fish jerking in its jaws.'—I mean, some things never change, right? You can just imagine this same conversation in Ancient Greece:

"(First General, Hysterically) 'Forget the wooden walls crap! An army of Spartans is gonna crawl right up my ass unless I get some straight answers now!'

"(Oracle, Blind and Gibbering) 'The chariots of Apollo burn, but are not consumed! The waves of destiny—'

"(First General) 'Ah, screw it. Stuff the old bag in the catapult and toss her over the walls. Who knows—maybe she'll explode when she hits the ground.'

"Thank you, you've been great!"

Sarah flopped down at the kitchen table.

"Four and a half minutes," Mother said, squinting

through bifocals at the second hand on her watch.

Sarah groaned. "Oh God. I need another minute and a half of material. I'm going to die. Take me now, Lord."

"Ancient Athens goes down big on the club circuit, eh?"

Sarah slumped over the table, her cheek propped on one hand. "Yeah, I know. Cursed by growing up with Dad, I guess. I take it you don't think the Peloponnesian Wars will get big yuks from my drunken admirers."

Mother tilted her head to one side. "I might be inclined to wait for the mini-series."

"*With Your Shields Or On Them,*" Sarah suggested. "Brought to you by Trojan Condoms. When you think 'forcible abduction,' think Trojan!"

"Eh? What's that?" Father called from the parlor.

"Nothing, Dad. Just taking the name of Thucydides in vain."

" 'Great is the glory of the woman who occasions the least talk among men,' " Father retorted, " 'whether of praise or of blame.' "

"When we were first married," Mother said dryly, "it was 'Silence gives the proper grace to women.' "

"Greeks: Ugh. God knows what those lovable old sodomites meant, but they sure did sound good."

Catching her mother in a snigger of complicity, Sarah thought, Well, now's as good a time as any other. A nervous shakiness rushed through her. Stage fright and lack of sleep, she told herself. Nothing she couldn't handle. Here goes. "So. Aunt Sophie not feeling well this morning? She's usually up by now."

"I'm not sure," Mother said carefully. "I haven't seen her."

"There was some kind of a fuss yesterday, wasn't there? The screaming tipped me off; I'm subtle that way. Why the hysterics over Dante's ring?"

Mother put her coffee cup down on the kitchen table. "I believe it may have looked like a different one," she said. "One your aunt gave someone a long time ago."

"Her husband?" Sarah asked casually.

Mother frowned. ". . . Yes."

"What was his name?"

"Pendleton," Mother admitted. "Percy Pendleton. The Third."

"So what happened to him? Why don't you guys ever talk about him?"

For a moment Sarah feared she had gone too far, but finally Mother shook her head and said, "It was a long, long time ago, and it didn't end well. It's not something we like to think about." She paused, as if judging what to say, or how much. "He disappeared about the time Dante was born. Your father thinks he committed suicide, but it's more likely he just ran off. I trust you know your aunt well enough to imagine her feelings in either case. It must have been a shock to her, to see Dante pull something out of the river that looked so much like Pendleton's wedding ring."

"A square ring?" Sarah protested. "That isn't too much of a coincidence? Or maybe there was a square ring fad they never taught me about in school."

For once Mother seemed to lose a little of her poise. "It can't be the same ring, Sarah. That was thirty years ago."

Whoa now—no point in spooking Mom before we get to the good stuff, Sarah reminded herself. She shrugged and nodded, pretending to agree. "Did Aunt Sophie ever think about having kids?"

Mother carefully added honey to her tea. "Yes," she said at last. "Yes, they thought about it."

Did more than that, Sarah thought. But what did she expect her mother to say: *Your aunt gave birth to a monster? Your aunt gave birth to a lovely boy, but he was stolen and Jet was left in his place?* It was a miracle they had kept Jet at all, Sarah realized. Knowing her aunt, she was surprised Sophie hadn't strangled him, or dropped him in the river.

Sarah shuddered, shook her head, and forced herself to get back to business. So who saved him, who saved little Jet? Was it her mother, moved by some compassionate impulse for the foundling? Or was it Father, who would keep Jet in the house for the same reasons he kept a skull on his desk?

To have your baby, your precious baby lost, and get a . . . thing, in its place. How horrible. How horrible.

"Sweetie?" Mother said, alarmed. "You're crying."

Sarah shook her head. "My eyes are just watering," she said unconvincingly. Lack of sleep was making her spinny, damn it. She was starting to let herself think about things she didn't think about. Ever.

She felt her mother's hand close over her own. "It's okay, sweetie. You'll have yours."

"I'm twenty-eight and fat, Mom. I haven't gotten a single call on my ad in *Millionaire's Weekly,* and the Beijing White Brides catalogue returned my picture with a form letter."

Mercifully the phone rang, giving Sarah an excuse to get out of the conversation before she said something that would hurt both of them even more.

She jumped to get it. ". . . Oh, my God—really? Of course. As soon as he gets in. And he should . . . Okay. Yeah— Yeah. Okay . . . Okay, thanks for calling."

Slowly she put down the phone and looked at her mother. "That was Dante's friend Laura," she said, absently wiping her eyes with the back of one hand. "He's supposed to call the cops; someone broke into his apartment last night."

It took Dante almost half an hour to fill the grave. Jet offered to help, but Dante shook his head and did it himself, shoveling the dirt back, tamping it down, covering it with dead leaves and ferns. Ashes to ashes, dust to dirt.

Seven more days, he thought.

Six and a half.

When he was finished, he said, "So what will you do when I'm gone?"

Jet shrugged. "I don't know. We'll be okay."

"Ha! Sarah may be fine, but you? Give me a break. I could blow you out like a birthday candle." Dante stowed the shovels back in the boat, next to his rod and reel. The magic lure still dangled on the end of his line, hooked carefully to the first eyelet.

Odd. He hadn't remembered bringing that stuff.

Dante glanced over at the willow, contemplating the strips where Aunt Sophie had sliced away its bark. They gleamed like the welts of a penitent.

Jet said, "You remember when Sarah ran away? Her sophomore year. A loathsome bastard with a headband. Lawrence."

"Father mentioned it. God, where was I? Why didn't

I come pound the shit out of him and warn him away from my sister like a big brother should?"

"At the time you were pursuing a life of torrid frivolity," Jet said dryly. "You had just escaped from University."

"You sound like a disapproving butler."

"I heard— I happened to overhear her once, talking to Mother," Jet said uncomfortably.

"You are a little spy, aren't you?"

Jet shrugged. "I didn't get that much, but it was clear that—something happened, just before she ditched him. I'm not sure what. But whatever it was, it hasn't gone away, Dante. She's still hurting."

Dante nodded thoughtfully. "What ever happened to Lawrence, anyway? I don't remember him bothering her after that."

"I killed him."

Dante blinked. "You're joking, right?"

"Of course," Jet said with a small, careful smile.

Jet gestured at the boat. "After you, sir?"

"Mm—I b'lieve not, my good man." Dante lifted his fishing tackle from the boat. "Take the rowboat back and clean it up for me, there's a good fellow. I feel a sudden urge to drop a line into the river."

Jet looked at him curiously. "Got a tip about a good spot?"

Dante began ambling along the shore. "I think I'll try up here beneath the fort. I fancy there might be something skulking in the willow pool."

Slowly Jet nodded. "Earn your wings, Clarence. Earn your wings."

Of course this is madness, Dante told himself as Jet

putted out into the channel. To deliberately take the lure, of all things, and drop it down under the big tree as his dreams had directed: this was sheerest angeling.

He could feel the white wings of magic opening around him.

But angeling was what the times seemed to demand. And besides, Dante thought mordantly, even if he went crazy, it would only be for a few more days.

His leather jacket was damp, its gorgeous stencils smeared with mud and crumbles of dead leaves. His fingers were getting stiff with the cold, and he wished he'd brought a pair of gloves.

He took his rod and reel and found himself a spot under the old willow, sitting on a great black root, thick as his waist, that boiled out of the ground at its base. The river had eaten the ground below it; sitting on the root, Dante swung his feet, watching his loafers just skim the water.

It was a dark morning. The sun toiled behind sullen masses of dark gray cloud. A thin mist still hung upon the river; here and there it thickened into cloudy ghosts that drifted sadly by him, like mourners in a funeral procession. Autumn's fire had swept down the valley, leaving the trees on the north shore bare. On the south side, shadowed from the sun, the maple trees still burned in time, each leaf a week-long twist of flame. Occasionally a crack would open in the clouds overhead, and a shaft of sunlight, glancing down, would kindle the maple leaves, or reveal a strange and sudden beauty in a length of whiskey-colored river.

It had been a long time since Dante had tasted sleep; his whole body ached for it. How voracious the stupid body is, he thought. Less than a week to live (please,

please, at least six more days!), horror and wonder on every side, and all the body can think about is sleep. And breakfast. Less than five hours had passed since he had opened a slit in his own dead belly and already his mind was starting to daydream about bacon and toast and hot coffee. Coffee! Loaded with milk and sugar, warm between his fingers . . .

Dante brought himself back with a jerk. What a bastard underhand trick, he thought savagely, looking down at his body. I'm still as smart as I ever was. Smarter! Sharp as a tack. Well-read. Funny. Good conversation. But everything I am sits here condemned, fastened to a dying animal.

A magpie flapped by, squawking, *eat! eat! eat!*

Biscuits, Dante thought. Hot white biscuits, gilded with margarine.

Casting his line into the river with a thin hissing whine, he saw his life writ large: the lowering sky full of dark portents, and shot through with gleams of dreamlike beauty. Slowly he reeled in the lure, filled up and overflowing with the mystery of the river, his hunger and the sullen clouds, memories and the mist; unexpected floods of light.

The lure jerked; snagged; pulled free. The line was heavy. As the lure came up to the surface, Dante saw its barbs swaddled in a rag of rotten cloth. He pulled it dripping from the water, and saw the cloth was tangled around something like a flat stick or splinter. Dante picked it up, turning it over in his fingers. It was small, perhaps an inch long, and white.

It looked like a human bone.

"And lo," he murmured. "I am become a fisher of men."

> I WOULD FAR RATHER BE IGNORANT, THAN
> WISE IN THE FOREBODING OF EVIL.
>   —AESCHYLUS

CHAPTER
SEVEN

DANTE'S FIRST CHORE WHEN HE GOT IN WAS TO track down Sarah and find out what she had learned from Mother about Aunt Sophie's long-vanished husband, Pendleton.

Then it was time to deal with the bone.

Starting with the guess that it was part of either a foot or hand, Dante snuck into his father's study and tracked it down with the aid of Gray's *Anatomy*. It turned out to be the first metacarpal of the upper extremity—the bottom of the thumb. Following Gray's advice to hold the bone with "the carpal extremity upward and the dorsal surface backward," Dante located "the tubercle for the extensor ossis metacarpi pollicis"—which faced right. Thus: the right thumb.

"Aha!" he murmured triumphantly, slowly closing the book. Then he froze, locked in memory as if in ice.

It was a long, still afternoon and he had wandered into his father's study. Light slanted through a narrow window, making lustrous the dark cherrywood desk and the white skull. Light glinted on the glass cabinet in which Father kept his medicine: rows of dark green bottles, shiny steel implements, the arthritis charms his patients had begun to ask for ("Well, placebos are good medicine too," he had sighed, swiftly knotting bits of willow-bark and colored ribbon as if tying a fly). His funny-looking pre-War baseball glove from high school and an untouched bottle of Courvoisier Five-Star he'd bought on graduation to drink the day he retired. The study was rich with Father's smells: shaving lotion and hair cream, perhaps a faint hint of the finger of whiskey he drank here after dinner each night. Everywhere the dense smoldering aroma of pipe smoke.

Dante liked pipe smoke better than the acrid stink of Aunt Sophie's cigarettes, but it was the scent of fresh tobacco that made him drunk. He loved to sneak into the study and open the second drawer of Father's desk, rooting through thickets of pipe reamers to uncover a glorious treasure: Amphora tobacco, packed in brown plastic pouches that felt and smelled like softest leather. When he found one he would open it like a Christmas present and hold it to his face, breathing its scent into himself until the room went dizzy.

But to get to his father's desk, Dante had to pass the medicine cabinet, its second-lowest shelf a rack of picks and saws and scalpels. And across the room, turned face out on the oak bookshelf, the dreadful Gray's *Anatomy*. This fat volume of bodies was the chief and lord of Grown-Up Books, full of his father's terrible secrets.

A hundred times he stood hovering in the doorway while Grandfather Clock ticked slowly behind him. Would the lure of the tobacco draw him into his father's terrible world? Or would wiser instincts prevail, and send him away from the dreadful book with the Skinned Man on the cover? His father had caught him once, and made him look into the Book; showed him a picture of the human heart and told him what it did.

That afternoon, sent upstairs for his afternoon nap, Dante had been lying with one arm sprawled over the edge of his bed. It was a hot stuffy summer day. The mattress was shaking with his heartbeat, shaking, thudding against his chest until he jerked his dangling arm back into the bed, terrified his heart would wear out from having to drive the blood up from his hanging hand. Every time he made his heart work he was wearing it out. The ugly lump of muscle his father made him look at in the dreadful Book: the traitor heart that one day would make him die.

Portrait

From the time we were seven years old, Father took us out once each fall to hunt. He didn't want us to forget where the meat we ate came from; didn't want us to think it grew in bloodless shrink-wrapped packages for our consumption.

This is a picture I took on Thanksgiving morning the year we were both twenty. In the foreground, framed by

Father's standing figure on one side and a thin silver birch on the other, you can see Dante's kill, a three-year-old buck. Blood drenches its throat where Dante's bullet hit, and spatters the innocent snow.

Dante is crouching just behind the buck. He is holding his rifle with the walnut stock planted between his knees, and his hands wrapped around the barrel.

It's one of the best black and whites I ever took, so sharp you can see the coils of Dante's breath, and the blood smoking at the buck's throat. You can almost hear the crackle of dead leaves underfoot.

No picture I have of them shows the resemblance between Dante and Father more strikingly. In life, Dante's energy fools you; you get distracted by his restless pacing, his flaring eyebrows, his darting hands. But in the picture he is still. He has taken Father's stillness into himself and you see his hands are Father's careful hands, thicker and more steady than mine. He has Father's gently rolling shoulders, and most of all he has Father's eyes. Without Dante's mobile face and flying brows to distract you, you see the same narrow blue eyes, deadly serious; the same quiet intensity.

Dante refuses to see any similarity between his father and himself. Father must wonder about this. I do. It seemed so obvious to everyone that Dante was destined to be Anton Ratkay's special child, the same way Sarah was her mother's. And yet somehow Dante drifted away: first arguments, then silence, then amiable banter; charming and meaningless and utterly impenetrable.

If you catch Father looking at Dante when he thinks himself unobserved, you can see the bafflement in him. In the depths of those eyes, long since steeled to bitter

*things, you can see him hurting, wondering when destiny
failed and he lost his son. Wondering what he should
have done ... what he could have done differently.*

*In the picture Dante looks intently at the dead buck
in front of him. There is no shock, no lip-trembling remorse; just the slightest narrowing of his narrow blue
eyes and a still intensity in his body as he ponders the
thing he has made.*

*Off to the side, Father is looking at Dante with exactly
the same expression.*

"Dante?"

Startled, Dante looked up to see his father standing in
the doorway of the study. He scrambled to his feet and
tucked Pendleton's thumb bone quickly in his shirt
pocket, next to the lure he had meant to return. "Sorry!"

Dr. Ratkay allowed himself a faint smile. "No problem
at all." He ambled over and tapped with one finger on
Gray's massive *Anatomy.* "Heavy, isn't it? More than
twelve hundred pages, and all the writing extremely
small."

They stood side by side. His father hadn't had the
grace to go bald yet, Dante noted with a twinge of envy,
though since last Christmas his salt-and-pepper hair had
become mostly salt. Looking down at the top of his father's head, Dante was struck by how Anton Ratkay had
begun to shrink: his shoulders were curling and his chest
was thinner. In the bulky brown sweater Aunt Sophie
had knit for him he seemed oddly old and frail, as if
bundled against a cold only he could feel.

Stooping over his desk, Dr. Ratkay coughed repeatedly—but into his hand, like a gentleman.

"You shouldn't smoke so much."

Father laughed, digging out his trusty briar and a pouch of Amphora. "Your mother says my face is turning into a tobacco leaf: all wrinkled and leathery. I try to tell her it's been pickled in aftershave, but she won't listen."

He tapped the *Anatomy* with the stem of his pipe. " 'Life is short, the art long, opportunity fleeting, experience treacherous, judgment difficult.' Hippocrates said that. It's still true, every word."

He dropped into the Radetzky swivel chair before his desk. As a rule he preferred to live with the furniture he had inherited from his parents, but he was a pragmatist. A few years after the new contouring synthetics came out, his back had begun to give him problems. Mother convinced him to give the Radetzky a try. "Think of it as research into the effectiveness of a new therapy for back pain," she said crisply. "If it works, you can suggest it to your patients."

"And warn them off the damn things if it doesn't," he'd grumbled, but the argument had been good enough. (And as Mother tartly observed, it hadn't hurt that Radetzky himself was Hungarian on his father's side.)

Ruminatively Dr. Ratkay pulled a fingerful of shredded tobacco from the pouch of Amphora. "Things change in medicine, of course, but not the central thing." Dante raised his eyebrows. "People die," his father answered, with a small rueful smile.

Dante shelved the Book, feeling a stab of pain from his abdomen, like a bad stitch. "I guess they do."

Dr. Ratkay frowned at the pipe mug, puzzled. "Hum. I wonder what happened to—"

Hastily Dante pulled the lure from his shirt pocket. "I took it out yesterday, to fish. I was just going to put it back."

Dr. Ratkay's eyebrows rose. "Quite a catch you made with it, too. That ring." He tamped down his wad of tobacco and struck a match. Shredded leaves flamed, blackened, burned. He sucked pleasurably and exhaled a cloud of blue-gray smoke.

Dante couldn't help grinning. I should get him a Chinese lounging robe, he thought. He would make a perfect scholar-dragon, a gently steaming mandarin lazing amid his hoard of books. Behind the smoke those eyes, still as bright as blue sky in winter.

His father examined him. "You know," he began, releasing the pipe with a small *pop* and a puff of smoke, "you are the same age now I was when you were born."

They pondered this in silence for a moment, Dante standing awkwardly with his hands in his pockets, his father seated, with his legs crossed and two fingers over the black briarwood bowl of his pipe. "I guess I don't measure up," Dante said lightly. "No wife, no kid, no degree. Hardly a job."

"True," his father conceded with a smile, "but not what I was thinking."

"Enlighten me."

Dr. Ratkay drew on his pipe. He blew a long slow stream of smoke into the air. Where it crossed the sunlight falling through the narrow window, it shone.

"When you have a child," he said at last, "it brings a lot of grief." He held up a hand. "Not the child's fault: at the worst the child brings exhaustion, bad temper . . . dry-cleaning bills." He shot a glance at Dante, reliving a distant memory. Thoughtfully Dr. Ratkay rubbed his chin. " 'Fathers are children for the second time,' as Aristophanes almost said. When you have a child, you see in him yourself as a child. That's part of what you love in him, you see. You love yourself, your younger self. And when you look at him and worry, you do it because you think of all the things you lost, growing up. All the hurt . . . " He stopped himself, blinked and smiled. "So now, looking at you, you fine, tall, smart young man, I can see all the mistakes I'm going to make with you and your siblings, *and* your aunt, *and* my practice, *and* God knows your mother."

"You? Make mistakes? I thought it was impossible!"

Anton smiled. "I did too, at your age. That was pretty old to be so foolish!"

"Whereas I know I hardly ever do anything right," Dante said. "I must be exceedingly wise."

Anton shook his head, looking sadly at his son through a haze of blue smoke. After a long silence, he said, "No. You're an even bigger fool than I was."

"Dad seemed a little glum tonight," Sarah remarked to her mother after dinner that evening.

Mother shrugged. Sleeves rolled up to her elbows, she pulled the last few scraps of meat off the turkey's ribs and tossed its skeleton in the garbage. Beside her, Sarah sighed and pulled on an apron, looking over the usual wreckage of dishes Saturday dinner had left in its wake.

"I've never seen your brother carve with such a . . . scientific interest," Mother remarked.

Sarah started water running in the sink and added a

healthy shot of detergent. Aunt Sophie had a deep aversion to dishwashers, which was fine, but as she had retired to her room after dinner, feeling unwell, it left Sarah with a depressing collection to do by hand. "We ought to get the boys in here to help."

Mother laughed. "Jet and Dante did most of the cooking while you snoozed upstairs this afternoon, you lazy thing."

"Yeah, I know." Resigning herself to the inevitable, Sarah rolled up her sleeves and began to scrub. She still felt hungry, but her reflection in the kitchen window told her she had eaten too much.

She hated it.

It was dark now. The lowering clouds had finally made good on their promise; rain creaked and spattered on the kitchen window, running in sudden tear-tracks down the glass. Sarah felt dull and melancholy. Two hours of fitful sleep, snatched in the mid-afternoon, had not made up for the horrors of last night's autopsy. Even Saturday dinner had been subdued: Aunt Sophie grim and moody, Father terse and withdrawn.

Mother clinked and clattered about the kitchen, determinedly cheerful. "When's your next show?"

"Tuesday night at Yuk-Yuks." As Sarah reached to fish another greasy plate out of the dishwater, her eyes involuntarily jumped to the window. Something had moved.

Something had moved outside.

She squinted, trying to see into the rainy night, but it was bright in the kitchen, and the window was crowded with reflections.

Once, years before at a darker time in her life, she had
lain in bed in an apartment downtown, listening to the
sound of faint screaming, very far away; it had run down
her skin in tiny tracks of fear, like cold water. Tonight,
straining to see through her own reflection, she felt the
same fear sliding coldly down her face.

She leaned forward until her forehead touched the
glass, looking through her own reflected eyes. Her heart
was racing. Yes—there! Down at the bottom of the
wilted garden, not far from the dim bulk of the boathouse.

Wasn't there a child, a little girl, staring up at the
lighted window?

Staring in at the warm house from the cold and the
rain; a child in jeans and a white T-shirt. A scrap of a
girl with water dripping from the brim of a baseball cap.

With a little cry Sarah dropped the plate she had been
washing. It smashed as she leapt to the back door, pulled
it open, banged through the screen door and ran down
the porch steps.

Outside the air was huge and full of night. Sarah faltered and stopped. Cold drops of rain spattered against
her face.

Nothing. No one.

She took a few halting steps down through the garden.
No one waited for her there. No sad little face re-
proached her from the shadows beneath the boathouse
eaves.

The wind sighed around her, and the rain wept. Still
Sarah walked, heart pounding and pounding in her chest.
She did not let herself think. This was not a time for
questions. She could only run; into the night, or away

from it. Those were her choices. She had made the wrong choice once, eight years before. She knew she couldn't bear to live if she made the wrong choice again.

The clouds stretched on forever; the thin breeze gusted and fell. Down beyond the slowly creaking dock, the dark river rolled on.

"Sarah? Honey—are you all right?"

Her mother stood in the doorway, calling to her. Warm yellow kitchen light spilled across the porch, and it was Sarah, Sarah who now stood, forlorn, in the shadow of the boathouse. From here the house looked unimaginably remote, warm and friendly and utterly inaccessible, having nothing to do with the rain whispering off into eternity around her. Nothing to do with the river, and the rolling darkness that covered everything real.

Soaked and shivering, Sarah watched her mother pick her way down through the garden. "A rabbi, a Baptist preacher, and a Roman Catholic priest are out walking one day when they meet the angel Gabriel," Mrs. Ratkay said, as soon as she was close enough for Sarah to hear.

"The rabbi says, 'Oy! Just who I wanted to see! I have here a list of complaints for you to take to the Master of the Universe.' And he takes out a book about a thousand pages long and gives it to Gabriel, and Gabriel says, 'As you wish.'

"Then the preacher says, 'Hallelujah! Praise be! I need you to take this petition singing the praises of Christ Almighty down to Hell. We're going to shame the devil! As you can see, it's been signed by over a million viewers— uh, that is, members of the congregation.' And he too takes out a book about a thousand pages long, covered in signatures. And Gabriel says, 'Very well.' "

Mrs. Ratkay put her arm through her daughter's arm and began to lead her gently up toward the house. "Well, that leaves the priest, who's looking kind of embarrassed. He hems and haws for a while, and shuffles his feet, and runs a finger around his clerical collar, and finally mumbles, 'Thanks for coming,' and stuffs a tiny slip of paper into Gabriel's hand. The angel picks it up and reads it, and a sudden change comes over him. His teeth start to chatter and his knees begin to knock. 'You're crazy!' he says, and dropping the slip of paper he flies shrieking into the night.

"Well, of course the rabbi and the preacher are amazed," Mother continued, guiding Sarah up the porch steps. "They stare at the priest so hard, he finally grins a feeble grin and says, 'A letter from me to the Pope, asking if we could ordain women.' "

Sarah almost smiled. "—And then the rabbi and the preacher also fly shrieking into the night," she whispered.

Gwen Ratkay led her daughter into the kitchen and sat her at the table while she put on a kettle. She took Sarah's hand. "Are you okay? I see little teapots behind your eyes, brewing tears."

Sarah couldn't laugh. It was too dark outside, too dark and cold; and the sad rain dripped and crept over all the earth. "Eight," she whispered.

Gwendolyn's eyes closed, her shoulders sagged, and for a brief moment she looked very old. "Shh," she murmured, softly stroking her daughter's hand. "It's okay, sweetheart. It's okay."

Sarah shook her head, furious. "She would have been eight years old," she cried. And wept and wept.

*   *   *

In the kitchen, Sarah cried while her mother gave her what comfort she could. In his study, Dr. Ratkay smoked and, sighing, painted a charm for the Gregson girl, who was young enough to hope it might somehow cure her baby's leukemia. Upstairs, Aunt Sophie bent over her sewing table, studying a pattern of coins with an expression both wondering and resentful, unable to believe what she saw prophesied in their fall.

Jet and Dante were talking softly in the parlor, where Grandfather Clock wove his steady, ceaseless spells against the dark night and the spattering rain. Red light flickered in his glass heart from the fire that hissed and creaked on the hearth. Dante jabbed moodily at the fire with a brass poker. It blazed and burned. Hungry flames caught; held; flowed in blue streams up the pale sides of the naked wood. Little red tongues licked black streaks onto it, burning it up, burning it away, burning it down into embers and ashes.

"What are you thinking?" Jet asked.

Dante blinked and shook his head. "Nothing. Everything." The bones of the human hand; Jet carefully rolling up the bamboo walls of their fort and storing them in the boathouse; the willow tree, its welts gummed with sap; dirt falling by the shovelful over his own face; the white sac webbed around his kidney and liver.

Maple leaves, burning down into winter.

"Someone broke into my apartment last night, you know. Laura called." Wearily Dante rubbed his eyes. "The cops think the guy was looking for something."

"What! Someone broke through the Crimson Bands of Cytorrak and penetrated the Sanctum Sanctorum! It must have been Baron Mordo!"

Dante laughed. "Or the Dread Dormammu!" Slowly his smile faded. "I can't imagine what anyone would want from my apartment. I don't even have a turntable."

Jet shrugged. "A maniac with a thirst for ugly white furniture, perhaps."

"I've never heard Laura sound so worried before. She probably said a prayer over my lock or something."

Jet said, "It's coincidence, no doubt."

"What is?"

Jet glanced at Dante, shaggy black eyebrows raised. "Someone breaking into your apartment the exact same night you discover your own dead body."

Dante stared bleakly into the fire. "Well, shit."

Time passed. Dante poured out the shot of whisky he had been promising himself all day, and another for Jet. Dante detested the way lesser Scotches blew up like firecrackers in his mouth; but the Glenlivet sank smoothly back to detonate like a depth charge deep in his chest, sending ripples washing through his whole body.

"Hm—good." Jet shivered and grinned, looking into his glass. "You know how I got the name 'Jet'? Short for 'jetsam.' Something tossed up by the river. Father's idea, of course. Something salvaged from the rushes."

"It could have been worse," Dante pointed out. "They could have named you Moses."

His foster-brother laughed.

Dante rubbed his temples. With his flaring eyebrows, it made him look like a weary Satan. "Jet, I have no damn idea what to do next."

"Let us consider." Putting down his whisky, Jet steepled his fingers and pursed his lips, looking for all the

world like a spidery Sherlock Holmes, his cheek marked
with a lascar's tattoo for undercover work in an opium
den. "Have we hit upon a method for angeling yet?"

"We?" Dante regarded Jet unenthusiastically. "Yes, I
suppose 'we' have."

"In what does it consist?"

"Carefully identifying the most horrifying course of action and then taking it," Dante said morosely. "Like
playing leapfrog with porcupines, or bobbing for apples
in a vat of acid."

"Dating Amalia Jensen."

"Shut up."

Jet smirked. "And what have you got to work with?
Things I mean, not ideas."

"What?"

"Like the mirror in your bureau. Places with magic in
them."

"Oh." Dante nodded. "Uh, okay. Pendleton's ring. His
thumb bone. The willow tree. The bureau mirror. The
lure."

"Anything else?"

"Not that I—Oh. Gray's *Anatomy*," Dante said
slowly. (His father's voice: "The autopsy is the third
movement of a sonata: the body, the living, the body
reconsidered.")

Jet looked at him sharply. "You're thinking again.
Good. Anything else?"

"Grandfather Clock, I suppose. But that's different."

"Is it? Why?"

"It isn't horrible," Dante said. "I don't know. It's just
different. Closer . . . closer to the center of things."

He bared his teeth around another shot of whisky, felt

it slide down his throat like smoke, drifting into his stomach and lungs and into his blood, billowing through the chambers of his beating heart, loosening him inside.

The angel in his belly stirred.

Jet's father would have sat in this parlor before the fire, Dante thought. Pendleton too would have had his life sliced into sections one second long by Grandfather Clock, that meticulous pathologist; each second a reflection mounted on the clock's glass casement for study, as on a slide.

It was obvious that he must have drowned: the ring and the thumb bone were clear evidence of that. Pendleton's living, the flow and flux of it, was lost forever when his lungs filled with river water. But the facts, the body reconsidered: Was it possible Dante might have enough of these to discover Pendleton's story? Reconstruct it, as a paleontologist could reconstruct the lifestyle of a prehistoric man from a single jaw or a couple of teeth?

"We know some things about magic in general," Jet said. "Ritual: ritual is good."

"There isn't exactly a liturgy for this."

"Not yet." Jet grinned. "You'll think of something. But a certain solemnity, a certain privacy . . . Where would the best place be? The boathouse?"

"Not on my life," Dante said.

"What's wrong with it? It's isolated, it's big enough. It has a little extra numen from the autopsy, I should think."

"It's also cold and damp," Dante said. "I don't intend to sit around freezing my ass off. I need my concentration," he added, with all the dignity he could muster.

Jet acquiesced. "Okay, how about your room? On the

bureau, in front of the mirror."

A serpent of dread slid down Dante's spine. He sighed. "Yeah, that's the place."

Jet glanced at Grandfather Clock. "We can just manage to start by midnight, if we hustle."

"Oh God, Jet, can't I at least take a nap? My eyes keep crossing ~~d my hands won't stop shaking."

Jet shook his head. "You want to see visions, remember? That's why the Indians used to fast and go without sleep until the gods sent them dreams. Come to think of it, we shouldn't have let you eat any dinner."

Dante whimpered.

He buried his head in his hands, and let sleep wash over him for one delicious moment before regretfully opening his eyes. "I won't let you down."

"I know."

"You must think I . . . Well, who the hell knows what you think? But I won't let you down."

"I know."

He found Jet looking at him with calm certainty. "I know. I would die for you, if I had to. You would die for me."

Dante drained the last of his whisky. "I may yet have that opportunity."

Fifteen minutes later he sat before the bureau in his room, his hands curled around a mug of hot willow-bark tea.

It was nearly midnight and very dark. The only light came from a single emergency candle Jet had filched from the kitchen and set at the base of the mirror. Arranged before Dante on the bureau like surgical implements were

Pendleton's ring and thumb bone, the lure, Gray's *Anatomy*, and Dr. Ratkay's second largest scalpel. Even in plain daylight it terrified Dante to touch any of these objects. In the candle's dim flicker their outlines grew shadowy, and dread poured from them.

Grown-up secrets.

Unclean.

What they found out behind the barn. What waited in his belly. Ann-Marie Bissell, who ran off to the City when she was twelve years old. Duane: a little boy in a hot room, bedsprings creaking. His uncle's hand.

Death to touch. Death to know.

Dante's face in the mirror was pale and mottled. He tried to calm himself, but his chest was banded in iron and he could barely breathe.

A spider crawled out of the candleflame and scuttled into the shadows.

Dante yelled. The fear was like having a syringe of ice water plunged into his heart. For an endless instant he went completely numb.

Am I dead?

Am I dead?

He felt a hand on his shoulder. "Shh," Jet murmured. "Shh, Dante. It's okay. It's all right. We knew it was going to be like this."

"We?" Dante hissed savagely. "Who the fuck are *we*?"

He reached out impulsively and jammed Pendleton's ring on his wedding finger. It fit.

Something scuttled over the back of his left hand.

A shudder went through Dante's body like a spear. He

squeezed his eyes shut and clenched his fists until the trembling passed.

Some time later he remembered to breathe. The fumes from the willow-bark tea were bitter as regret.

In his mind's eye Dante saw the Skinned Man on the cover of Gray's *Anatomy*. The Skinned Man had nothing anymore. No life, no love, no hope, no regret—just a body. Dismantled man.

Dante groped in the shadows for Pendleton's thumb bone. He found it, held it for a long moment, and then, prompted by something he dared not examine, he dropped it into his mug of tea.

Let it steep.

He heard a sharp hiss of indrawn breath from Jet.

"Give me your hand," Dante croaked, his voice throttled in his cramping throat.

Jet's hand left his shoulder. "What?"

Dante held up the scalpel. "It's your story, damn you. Give me your hand!"

Slowly Jet extended his right hand. It was shaking. Good! Let the bastard sweat a little. Quickly Dante drew the scalpel across Jet's palm, a shallow cut. Blood beaded up along the incision. Dante tilted Jet's hand, and three red drops spilled into the tea.

Dante put the scalpel down. "We're ready to start," he said.

A first long sip of Pendleton, to get his subtle flavors.

Instinctively, Dante adopted his father's clinical persona, stepping into it like a surgical gown. It fit perfectly. Though he had never chosen to wear it, it must have been there inside him always, patiently waiting until he chose to draw it on.

So then: Pendleton's flavor as it rolled across the tongue. Salt and bitter both, but very little sweet. It had been the salt Sophie craved, the sharp tang of him. Tasting him again, as if through Aunt Sophie's lips, Dante noted a resemblance, stronger in her tasting than in his, between Pendleton and her father. But Dante's grandfather (the one to whom he owed his flaring eyebrows) had been a joker, a wise man, a magician born too soon to flower. What he loved was the wonder of his audience, its delight. For Pendleton there was a thinner savor: the thrill of conquest, of fooling people. He was a man of averages, of calculated risk.

Dante sat with eyes closed, Pendleton's ring on one hand and the other lying on the *Anatomy* as if it were a book of necromancer's spells. He took another sip of bitter water, steeped with willow bark and a human thumb. Blasphemy soaked into him like oil into dry wood. One part of Dante, cowering in horror behind his father's impassive, surgical mask, felt as damned as the first angel fallen. What madness had taken him, to turn his back on grace and plunge into the dark?

But Dante's time was short and his need great. His sharp steel intelligence flashed and bit into his family, peeling back its skin, looking always for Pendleton's story, following its course as he might note the progress of a cancer. All his life he had left certain silences unbroken, ignored certain cuts and bruises in his family's flesh. Now the things he had trained himself not to see were what he needed to examine. His own fear was his guide, fear of secrets and things best left unseen. Dread had closed like scar tissue over the wounds in his family, sealing them.

Where he found it, he cut.

CHAPTER
EIGHT

JET HAD BEEN WATCHING DANTE FOR WHAT SEEMED like ages. From time to time, lost in his strange angel's world, Dante would whisper unintelligibly, like a man talking in his sleep. Sometimes his eyes were closed. Other times they opened wide, staring into the candle-flame or gazing at things hidden deep within the mirror. Different expressions haunted Dante's face: fear, most often; sometimes anger, or bitter grief, or unhealthy curiosity. Occasionally his devilish eyebrows winged upwards in astonishment. At least once he laughed, making Jet jump like a startled cat.

For over an hour Dante had nursed his cup of tea, but now, whether he had sipped it all away, or followed some inscrutable impulse, he set the mug down, slowly as a blind man, and groped across the bureau until his fingers touched the fishing lure.

A friendly game.

There was a soft tap on the door. "Dante?" It was Sarah.

Quietly Jet turned the knob. "Surprise," he murmured.

"You again! What's going on?"

"An angel in converse with the spirit realms." Jet blinked the candleflame from his eyes until he could make out Sarah's pajama'd form, looming in the hallway like a white flannel ghost. "What brings you here, O specter of the night?"

"Couldn't sleep," she said shortly. "Or rather, the sleep was fine: it was the dreams I couldn't stand. I was going downstairs to get some hot milk and I thought I would see if anyone was awake."

" 'Anyone' meaning Dante," Jet murmured dryly. "I doubt you were looking for me."

"You don't have to be such a touchy bastard."

Sarah shuffled into the room and peered at her brother. Dante showed no signs of noticing either of them. "What has he got in his hand?"

"Fishing lure," Jet said. "It's tied up with Pendleton's story somehow."

The two of them at the table, Jewel's friend smiling, smiling. Jewel herself lying in the bed, wearing nothing but one of his shirts. Young, so smooth and young: it made him drunk to look at her, by God; it made the laughter bubble in his chest. And she would laugh back and prod him with one naked foot; she could just reach his chair from the bed. On the table by the pack of cards a glass of champagne, pale pale gold, and the bubbles rising in it like his luck. That's how it was. That's how it felt before the first deal.

"Pendleton, Pendleton," Jet murmured. "My father." Delicately, he licked his lips. "Curious. I don't believe I've ever said those two words in that particular order."

"What do you know about him?" Sarah whispered.

"He left," Jet said flatly.

During the long, uncomfortable silence that followed this reply they watched Dante stroke the back of the lure, lightly, with the fingers of his right hand. Finally he picked it up and held it before his eyes. It dangled over the candleflame, faintly jingling. Light gleamed on its carapace and glinted on its thin barbed legs.

A dead man's hand. Aces and eights: what Wild Bill Hickok was holding when they shot him in the back. Should be enough to win at stud, but somehow a shiver went through Pendleton as slowly he picked up his cards. It was hot in the room, but he was cold inside. Something trickled down his cheek, pale pale gold; as if he were sweating out the fine champagne, leaving him stone-cold sober, his face as gray as ashes.

What could happen? So he'd bet his firstborn son, so what? The joke was on the stranger; Pendleton didn't have a son to lose.

Wasn't going to either—not with Jewel.

He realized this suddenly, looking over. He had always seen how young she was, how fierce and alive. Always before, it had made him feel young too.

Not now. Now gray age streaked his fine black hair. It sat in his belly like a cold gray stone. Now he held a dead man's hand.

He lost his nerve at that moment, so cleanly he could hear the snap. He'd had a lot of nerve, once. He had followed Crowley like a textbook, mastered his tricks with countless hours of practice. Brought his will to bear, and made of illusion a careful science. "A wizard needs nerve," he'd told Jewel.

Pompous ass.

She had grinned like she was grinning now, utterly beyond him. He had made himself a wizard, but Jewel was an angel. Her generation had been born into this world of wonders. She talked to her dolls, she told him once, and they talked back. She never stopped to wonder at that. How amused she had been, at his surprise. How many times had he seen that look in her, that amused contempt? As many times as he had thrust it away, buried it, slicked back his graying hair and made grand promises of the miracles he would teach to her.

Him teach her! She would melt him like wax if he got too close.

She prodded him with her naked foot and laughed. She must know it was over for him. His nerve had broken and she must have heard the snap.

He stared down at his cards while cold sweat beaded on his forehead.

Aces and eights.

"Do you think Dante's really going to die?" Sarah murmured. "Soon, I mean."

"I hope not; we just got through burying him. It would be very inconsiderate of him to keel over while I still had shovel-blisters on my hands."

"Don't be flip, Jet. Not about this."

They stood together, watching Dante. Sarah stirred. "What about the larval sac?"

"Maybe there isn't one in his real body. Even if there is, it didn't give him any trouble before last night."

"But he thinks he's going to die."

"He's been running from himself for thirty years," Jet said. "Now he's facing himself at last and it's got him scared shitless. Just because he feels like he's going to die, that doesn't mean he will."

Sarah said, "Maybe it does, if you're an angel."

"It's not my fault!" Jet hissed. "God damn it, just because I made him take a look at his life, that doesn't mean I made the problem. The problem was there!"

"No one said it was your fault."

"He spends his whole life drinking and screwing while the world is falling to pieces around him, but the first sign of trouble and everyone looks at me. I'm the only one willing to tell him to get off his ass, that's all. I'm the only one to break the news he isn't living in a fairy tale."

Sarah's shrewd gaze flicked from Jet to Dante and back again. Jet turned away from her measuring eyes. Slowly Sarah nodded. "I see. You're scared shitless too."

And so, furtively, he tried to gather what will he had left and cast the little card spell that had once made him so proud. It had taken him months to learn, hundreds of hours of practice, visualizing with cards in his hand, flip-

ping back and forth through Crowley's books, concentrating until his mind felt like a dishrag. Jewel's Card, he called the trick. She laughed when he showed it to her.

But it had gotten him out of a few tight jams before. Bought them this pale gold champagne and paid for this hot room in a swank hotel, for that matter. He concentrated on the cards in his left hand, on the useless four of clubs.

Desperately hoping Jewel's friend wouldn't notice.

"I call."

Life emptied from his left arm like water suddenly draining from a sink, leaving his fingers cold and gray and lifeless. Shaking with fatigue, Pendleton laid his hand slowly on the table. "Full house," he whispered. Now instead of two pair and a four of clubs, he had two pair and the ace of diamonds. Jewel's Card. "Full house," he said again. "Aces over eights."

"Can you imagine it?" Jet murmured. "The whole pregnancy, all nerves and hope and hideous discomfort, and then labor, so agonizing you think you're going to die from the sheer pain—and for what? For nothing. Your baby ripped away and this . . . thing, left in its place. Worse than retarded because it isn't yours. And your husband's gone, and you're living on your brother's charity, and everyone knows." With thin white fingers Jet touched the butterfly on his cheek, traced the diamonds on its outspread wings. "Everyone knows."

Sarah said, "Shut up."

"I wonder why she didn't strangle me."

"Jet!"

"Or pop me in a sack and toss me in the river. At first

they wouldn't leave her alone with me—did you know that? Even so, she had her chances: but she never did it."

"You were still her child," Sarah said, her voice crushed down to a whisper. "That counts for something, you know. You can't imagine how much that means."

"I don't know. Was I her child?" Jet shook his head, strangely vulnerable. "What goes on in someone's heart? I don't know. I've watched you people, watched you all my life and I still don't know. It used to drive me crazy, wondering; wondering what you all were thinking, wondering what you were feeling. I gave up, in the end."

"Who are 'we'?" Sarah asked tartly. "Are you into your tiresome 'I'm not a member of the human race' thing again?"

Jet smiled thinly. "If it's tiresome for you, just think how tired it makes me."

"It's the act that counts, Jet. Whatever Sophie felt, she didn't strangle you. She could have, but she didn't. And I'm glad," Sarah added, awkwardly.

Softly, Jet laughed. "Yeah, you probably are, at least a little. I'm sorry. You have problems of your own. You don't need to listen to me being maudlin."

"Actually, it's sort of refreshing to hear you whine," Sarah remarked. "Usually you just complain about us. This makes you seem more—"

"Human?" Jet said dryly.

Sarah grunted. "Oh no, Jet. I'd never accuse you of that."

For the longest time, Jewel's friend didn't say a word. Just glanced from Pendleton's hand to his own. "Nice," he said at last. And slowly, very slowly, he folded his cards facedown on the table.

"Well, that's enough don't you think?" Pendleton babbled, leaping up. "Would you care for a little more champagne?"

"Two hundred years, was it?" Jewel's friend said. "Two hundred years of life I owe you."

Pendleton shrugged. "Oh well, whatever." His hand shook as he poured himself another tumbler of champagne. It went down like ice water.

"Think that's enough?" Jewel asked teasingly. "You won't be able to walk, let alone take me dancing."

"M-maybe you're right," Pendleton said. "Why don't you and, and—"

"Albert," Jewel suggested, laughing merrily. "Oh, definitely Albert."

"Fine. Why d-don't you and Albert go on ahead? I'll find you later. I—I just need a few minutes to let the buzz out," Pendleton stammered: but he had never been more sober, not in the six months he had known her. He was straight as a casket and sober as a corpse. "Don't, uh, don't worry about the bet," he added. "Just a friendly game, after all."

Albert smiled. Coolly, like a well-bred tiger. "I never forget my debts," he purred.

The instant they headed downstairs Pendleton packed, shoving a few clothes into his suitcase, leaving behind his gold studs and his sharp hat. His three Crowley books, their margins thickly scrawled with notes, he shoved into the elegant fireplace and sprinkled with fluid from his gold-plated cigarette lighter. They burned up like mothwings.

In ten minutes he was ready, struggling into his long

coat. Sweat stained his white silk scarf. Door or fire escape? Don't be a fool, he told himself. No point panicking now. They'll be in the ballroom. Even if she sees you, so what? Tell her you're going out for a pack of smokes.

Not the elevator: too cramped. Go down the stairs; you can dodge onto a landing if you hear footsteps.

He was stuffing his fine leather gloves into his cashmere coat pockets when his eye fell on the stranger's cards, still facedown on the table.

He stood as if paralyzed. Then, suddenly, he reached out and tipped them over.

A royal straight. Not a flush, but a five-card straight, good enough to beat any hand under a full house.

Pendleton's heart thudded painfully in his chest.

A royal straight. With the ace of diamonds at the top.

"Christ!" Sarah swore, staring at Dante.

Jet spun around, following her gaze.

Dante sat before the bureau mirror, rocking back and forth, eyes closed, lips pressed thin as if in pain. His right hand was curled into a fist around the barbed lure and he was squeezing, squeezing until his knuckles turned white. Blood welled between his fingers. "Dead man's hand," he whispered.

Portrait

Christmas 1960.

It's written on the back of the picture in Mother's neat round hand. A black and white shot, not in the best of condition. It looks bleached: the black has faded to gray, and the white border is yellowing. Even though I did not take this photograph, it is one of the most precious in my collection.

There are two couples standing in front of the fireplace: Gwen and Anton Ratkay on the left, Aunt Sophie and Pendleton on the right. The two women are seven and a half months pregnant; flanked by their husbands they stand in three-quarters profile so their bulging tummies almost touch.

Anton Ratkay's smile is strained. He is two years out of medical school, working like a demon to establish himself in a community that prefers to deal with old Dr. Thompson. Dr. Thompson is looking to ease into his retirement and has just thrown a bit of business Father's way. Starting in the New Year, he will turn over all the autopsy work.

It is almost impossible to believe that Mother was ever this pretty. Red bangs curl around her Scottish face. The morning sickness they said would end after the first trimester still lasts past lunchtime, but though you can see the weariness around her eyes, her expression is one of wit and resolute good cheer. She is twenty-six years old in this picture, the smart, pretty daughter of an Episcopalian minister. In a pinch she could still play Anne in Persuasion, *although pregnancy and five years of marriage have aged her too much to play Elizabeth in* Pride and Prejudice, *her favorite book to this day.*

Aunt Sophie's smile is radiant.

This hurts.

Aunt Sophie's smile is radiant because she is thirty-six years old and pregnant. Too colorful, too ironic, too eccentric for this provincial time in American history, she had resigned herself to becoming an old maid when Pen-

dleton burst into her life, proposing to her in the middle of her shift as a cocktail waitress at the Top Hat. She towers over Mother by six inches. Where Mother is wearing a white smock with sensible pockets, Sophie's dress is a fanciful chiffon thing with puffy sleeves, over which she wears one of her Hungarian vests, embroidered with a riot of giant flowers, violets and poppies and roses. She is holding her cigarette like a gangster and smiling like a movie star.

(Don't smoke! I scream inside. That's me in there! How dare you take such a risk? . . . But she doesn't realize, of course. It was a doctor who told her to take up smoking in the first place—to "calm her nerves." She intends to give her baby the best care in the world, feed it from the most hygienic bottles, take it to Europe to broaden its mind. Ecstatic to have made it this far through the pregnancy, she has never questioned her own impulse not to ask her coins about the baby. She barely notices her own unease when she thinks about the future.)

And Pendleton? A sharp-dressed man of forty with immaculate hair, dressed in a tux that makes Anton look dowdy in his cardigan.

Is it only knowing what I know now that makes me see ragged fear in Pendleton's eyes, in his brittle smile?

What happened?

Knowing he had cheated in his poker game with Jewel's Sending; knowing the Sending knew it; knowing that his firstborn child was forfeit, how could this have happened? How could he be standing by a pregnant wife at this time of life?

My guess is that she tricked him. Aunt Sophie was never one to let other people's wishes stand in her way.

How easy it would have been, to say she was barren, or had her tubes tied, or had an IUD in. A man's desire not to wear a condom always makes him gullible on such a score.

Sophie is radiant. Her smile rivets you; you can't look away from it.

I didn't find the picture by accident; it was Mother's doing. She found me in the parlor a week before the fateful Thanksgiving. I had just rolled up the fort to face another winter.

"I know you're interested in photographs," she said. "I was just putting my albums in order, and it occurred to me you might like to flip through some of these old ones." Her voice was casual, but her eyes were strangely serious; it struck me at the time.

It was no accident I found this picture. Mother wanted me to see it, to think about it.

What impulse moved her, I wonder? Did I look so forlorn that day, puttering around the fort—so lost without Dante? For some time I had been thinking about my place in the family. Inconspicuously, I had thought, but Gwendolyn has sharp eyes. Not much gets by her. It would be very much like her, to let the cat out of the bag indirectly and with minimal fuss, like one of Miss Austen's well-bred heroines.

Maybe she loves me.
These days, even miracles are possible.

Dante sat in front of the bureau mirror. Blood seeped from his clenched fist and trickled down his forearm.

"Oh, my God," Sarah cried, running to her brother. "Dante! Dante! Are you all right?—Get a bowl of water!" she yelled at Jet.

"What if that wastes everything, so he has to do it again—"

"Get me the damn water and a towel."

Jet stood quivering for a long, wordless moment, then ran from the room. Sarah clasped her brother's face between her hands. "Dante? Dante, look at me."

He blinked and shook his head. "S . . . Sarah?" He frowned, distracted, and looked down at his hand. "Ow, shit!" he yelped, opening his fist. The lure dangled from his hand, its hooks embedded in his palm and fingers. "Ow, shit, get it off! Get it off!"

"Sit still," Sarah snapped, studying the damage through narrowed eyes.

"Ow!"

She paused for a moment, bent down, and swiftly kissed the top of his head. "Idiot." Then she sighed. "Don't expect sympathy from me," she added, teasing out the first hook. "Anyone stupid enough to do this deserves what he gets."

Dante bit his lip to keep from screeching while Sarah worked the barbs free of his hand.

By the time she removed the last hook, slipping it from the flesh at the bottom of his thumb, Jet had returned with a basin of warm water and a tea towel. "Mother caught me," he muttered. "I told her we were up late talking. She said it was bloody late and if we wanted to chat we could bloody well do it in the kitchen."

Sarah grunted, dipping Dante's hand in the warm water. "Get some rubbing alcohol, would you? I think they still keep it in the medicine cabinet. If not, any kind of disinfectant will do. God knows where this lure's been."

"The mouth of a pike," Jet said with a grin that made his butterfly tremble. It faded into uncertainty at Dante's suddenly stricken expression. "Hey, D. What are you staring at?"

"Diamonds!" Dante reached up as if to trace them, etched on Jet's cheek. The butterfly's wings were a lace of diamonds. Sarah grabbed his hand and stuck it back in the water. "Jewel's Sending," Dante whispered. "His mark."

When Jet returned with the rubbing alcohol, Sarah soaked one corner of the tea towel in it. "This is going to sting," she said with grim satisfaction.

She was right.

When the wound had been cleaned and Dante had run out of swear words, she bandaged his injured hand. Then they crept down to the kitchen, where they could talk without disturbing their elders. "All those yips and whimpers!" Jet remarked to a sour-faced Dante. "You sounded like a poodle in a duck press."

"How'd you like your face pressed?" Dante growled.

"Are you going to have to do it again?" Sarah asked.

Dante stared blankly at her. "What?"

"Jet said you'd have to do it all over if we stopped you from mutilating your hand."

Dante regarded Jet unenthusiastically. "How thoughtful."

"It was a legitimate concern."

Dante's shoulders sagged. "Yeah. Yeah, you're right.

God knows I don't want to go back there."

(The sweat, trickling like ice water down his face as the stranger regarded his cards. The shock as his nerve snapped and he saw himself clearly for the first time in years, and saw he was not young. Saw that he would never be young again.)

(Jewel's eyes as bright and hard as diamonds.)

"I don't want to do that again." Dante wiped cold sweat from his forehead and winced as little needles of pain pricked his hand. He had sat before his mirror and read the squalid diary of another person's life. He felt old and corrupt.

"What were you doing?" Sarah asked.

"The same thing I've been doing for—God, what time is it? Past three!" Dante groaned. "Sleep! God, I need some sleep."

Five more days.

He knew, he knew, god damn it, but how could he put things right when he couldn't keep his eyes from crossing?

Five more days.

Dante sighed. "So I think I know a little more about what happened to Jet. Now we have to find an angel named Jewel."

But first I must sleep, Dante thought later, lying in bed after Jet and Sarah had gone. I've got to sleep.

He burrowed under his pillow. The bright light in his room kept him awake, but then it kept him from screaming in fear, too. Kind of a trade-off, there.

First thing in the morning, he and Jet would go looking for information on this angel, Jewel. Nothing would be open before nine on a Sunday; he could sleep until seven-thirty, with luck. That would leave him just over four and a half days.

Four and half days.

"Sleep! Sleep, god damn you!" Dante clutched his pillow with both hands and pulled it around his ears.

He couldn't breathe.

With a groan he sat up in bed and glared balefully at the bureau mirror. Nothing there but old marble facing, a few spatters of blood, the stub of a fat white emergency candle, and the reflection of a tousled balding puffy-eyed nervous wreck who could use a shave.

Dante groaned again and shambled over to the light switch like a zombie with a hangover. "Screw it," he mumbled, slapping it off. What could he imagine that would be worse than what he'd already seen tonight?

Lots.

He tried a small thought experiment and imagined a fat-bodied spider scuttling out of his own dead throat.

Big deal.

"Hoorah!" he muttered. He'd finally blown his terror fuse. He tumbled back into bed.

As for tracking down Jewel's friend, the man she had jokingly called Albert: that would be harder. Even if he could find Jewel, there was no guarantee she would have kept in touch with Albert.

Maybe they could pick up the scent at the hotel somehow. There couldn't be that many hotels that fancy in town; Dante was pretty sure he'd recognize the suite if he saw it, or one like it.

It's been at least thirty years, he reminded himself. All very well to talk about time as stored on slides one second thick, interchangeable, et cetera, but the hotel might have been torn down, or altered beyond recognition. The same might be true of Albert, for that matter.

Dante winced, squeezing his eyelids closed. Sleep! Sleep, you idiot! God, I feel like yesterday's meat loaf. Probably taste like yesterday's meat loaf, for that matter. Ugh. Got to get off this anatomy kick. There is more to life than the meaty organism.

Not much more. Not your life.

("Why not?" Jet had said. "You're almost done with it.")

Dante groaned and turned over again. All right. All. Right. And what do we do when we need to go to sleep? What do we do when we need to relax? he asked himself.

He gripped his penis with grim determination.

It flopped limply in his hand. Apparently there was something about being terminally ill and chronically terrified that took it out of the old libido.

Too bad, Dante thought sternly, rubbing away. The stupid body can make me tired and hungry, so it can rise to the damn occasion now.

There, he thought morosely, feeling the first stiffening tremor in his hand.

Now: Who? Gina from the next lab? Nah—too many times recently. Stephanie? No—too soon since she dumped me for that bookkeeper with the beard. Unnamed fourteen-year-old nymphomaniac with a ponytail and an urge to learn?

Dante winced, thinking involuntarily about what it would be like to get a blow job from someone wearing braces. Definitely not. Besides, too unsavory.

Something aggressive, appealing to the old rape in-
stinct? He shuddered. God, no. Not now. Nothing kinky,
nothing fierce. Nothing that touched any of the dark
places inside himself. Sometimes, OK—that was what
fantasy was for, after all. But not now. Christ. Not now.

Laura.

Dante sighed, relieved. Of course—Laura.

There was a definite stirring down below. All in favor
of the image of Laura, raise your hands.

Laura grinning, her short black bangs framing her long
Chinese face, those weird skyscraper earrings of hers
swinging. Laura in a kimono—did they wear kimonos in
China or was that just Japan?—laughing at him across
her grandmother's tea set. Her long body shadowed by
the fall of silk, doubly exciting because they'd known one
another so long without sleeping together.

Laura leaning forward in a whisper of silk, her eyes
open—yes, she would watch him, grinning. She wouldn't
close her almond eyes. She wouldn't be embarrassed by
the touch of his eyes on her. Laura leaning forward—

He was breathing rather rapidly now, as the bed
creaked and complained beneath him—

Laura leaning forward, with the silk lapels parting to
show the swing of a small brown breast, and he would
brush the tip of it with his fingers—

o yes—

And when they kissed, her thin lips would smile under
his, and he would cup the breast in his hand, and say,

o—

and say—

o! o! o!

Will you marry me! Marry me! Marry!
Aaaaaah!
Oh. Oh. Oooh ...

... At last, at last after three days he was drifting off, snuggled under his blankets with the warm weight of sleep rolling under and around him like a river. He was drifting, drifting, floating away. . . .

Marry me?

CHAPTER
NINE

PORTRAIT
This picture was crucial to my career. As the winning photo in a juried competition, it opened the way for me to get steady work as a freelancer for the City's two big newspapers. To my certain knowledge it also cost one man his life.

I spend a lot of nights away from home, walking through the city, seeing it in black & white. By day it is noisy, crowded, absurd with its seething millions. At night, against a stark black background, stories play out cleaner, and the great features of the city shadow forth: downtown with its continents and canyons; the river a ribbon of woods threaded through the City's heart, where tramps live in cardboard boxes or under plastic

135

bags strung from trees. Westwood like a garden, its houses planted in stately rows, Volvos sprouting from each driveway. Peter Street and The Scrubs: desolations of asphalt and broken glass.

There is a class of walkers who share a certain camaraderie. We are not drunks, tramps, hookers, cops, priests, party-goers or night-shift workers: we are merely outsiders. On the rare occasions when we meet we acknowledge one another with a tiny tilt of the head, or a quick nod; but each of us carries his or her own solitude. We are invisible and we cannot be touched.

In my particular case, my butterfly is a powerful charm. Many times it has granted me passage through neighborhoods no white man has any business visiting after dark. Talismans, walk-aways, voodoo men and hellmarks and the Five Signs: almost every charm that isn't Chinese has come out of the slums, and for good reason. They are sinks of rage and fear, and the magic festers in them. The cops and the government have pulled out without telling anyone, bit by bit, year by year, abandoning them to their own bad dreams. The housing projects of Johnson's Great Society are haunted now, and deadly. Nobody knows how many people the minotaurs take each year.

I have seen teenage boys who would have gunned Dante down without a thought back away from me with fear in their eyes and cross themselves like Catholics. A block off Peter Street on one of my frequent routes there is an old woman who leaves out three olives as an offering for me every night.

I've taken to eating them when I go by.

It was in The Scrubs that I took this picture of two

boys one night. Behind the body of a junked Camaro one is kneeling execution-style, his forehead on the road, his hands clasped behind his neck. The other boy is standing behind him with a gun, pressing the muzzle against the back of his victim's head.

It was three in the morning when I turned the corner and nearly walked into the execution. Everybody froze: me, the boy with the gun, the other members of the gang; everybody except for the victim, who was cursing quietly and continuously.

"Fuck." The boy with the gun stared at me in helpless fury. I stared at him the same way. He might have been fifteen.

He might have been fifteen years old and it was so unfair that I should have walked in on him at just that moment. So unfair that he should have to deal with a Visitation when he had other business.

I looked at him and I couldn't see a human thing.

Better people than I could have seen it in him somewhere, some spark of the Divine, but all I saw was a fifteen-year-old killer, a disgusting, unnatural monster. I would have crushed him like a scorpion if I could.

Instead I raised my camera to my shoulder, set the focus and squeezed the trigger, snapping shot after shot of him as he stood there with the gun in his hand. Shooting him again and again as his dumb rage grew, staring at me with utter hatred until his finger tightened and he blew out the other boy's brains, again and again, emptying nine rounds into his head, all the time looking at me, looking at me, knowing he was caught, knowing he was a dead man, and there was nothing he could do.

I would take the film to the police and he would go to

jail and there was nothing he could do about it. To him I was a magic thing, less human than the kid whose brains he had just spattered over the road. I was nothing but an instrument of his Fate.

The trial was quick and ugly and they made me testify. The prosecution moved to have the boy tried as an adult and the defense didn't bother to contest. The whole proceeding took forty minutes and the verdict was life.

I heard later he died in jail. They do a set of exams on each new inmate and he scored too high on the Angel Test. Supposedly the scores are confidential, but a jail is of all places the most horrible: when a minotaur comes into being, it doesn't distinguish between the inmates and the authorities. So somehow the Angel Test scores always leak, somehow a weapon finds its way into another inmate's hands, and somehow the killer is never caught.

I call the picture "Minotaurs."

Only we can't blame the magic for them. Magic is in all the headlines these days, like a fashionable disease, but it isn't the magic that fails to educate blacks and Latinos and poor white trash. It isn't the magic that keeps us from making a real commitment to creating decent jobs at decent rates of pay. It isn't the magic that makes four out of every five black boys grow up without fathers. The magic did not make the gangs; we made them ourselves.

These are not changelings: these are our children.

In black and white, I shot one dead.

Jet looked through the viewfinder of his camera like a sniper looking through a scope, fixing it on the pagoda in the middle of the carp pool behind the Twelve Dreams Episcopal Church. On a park bench beside him Dante sat with his head resting wearily in his hands. He stared at the clay-colored water littered with lily and lotus pads long past blossoming. From time to time one of them would tremble as a big carp passed by, cruising for bread crumbs.

Snap. Jet's camera whirred, advancing the film. "This is a truly rotten idea," he commented.

"The service will be over soon," Dante said stubbornly. "Then she'll come here to feed the carp. That's what she does on Sunday mornings."

"You've been here with her?"

"Well, no, but I'm sure that's what she said."

"What if it's too cold?" Jet sighed. "Look, D., I'm not trying to be a pain in the ass here. But by your own calculation you don't have a lot of time—"

"I'm aware of that, thanks."

"We should be doing something useful. Calling up the Angels' Guild, for instance."

"Then do it! There's a pay phone on the corner. Ask questions about Jewel. Be a detective. But I have to talk to Laura, okay?"

Jet grunted. "If you want my friendly advice, I don't think she's going to find this confession particularly endearing."

"Who the fuck asked you?" Dante snarled.

Jet shrugged and Dante looked away. Overhead the bright sun seemed utterly warmthless. Omens roiled in the cloudy gray water, making lily pads tremble.

Twelve Dreams Episcopal stood on the border between the seedy downtown core and the gentrifying Chinatown.

Redbrick buildings from the forties and fifties held herb-alists and ink-and-stamp shops, a credit union, a handful of bakeries, and a pair of butcher shops with pressed ducks dangling in their windows. Local radio stations advertised on tall billboards; just beyond the church fence, with its line of autumn-withered bamboo canes, the *New China Times* building rested from the labor of putting out its Saturday shopping supplement.

Jet studied the cityscape. "Laura's an architect, isn't she? Successful one."

"Mm."

"Ever wonder why she lives in a cheap little apartment in your building?"

"How the hell should I know?"

Jet continued to study the city skyline rising around them. "My point."

Dante scowled.

The *China Times* gong had just sounded noon when a stream of parishioners trickled from the church into the gardens. While old women in polyester pants stood chatting on the church steps, a pack of children raced along the winding paths to the little pagoda that jutted over the water. Here they sat teetering on its bamboo rails and slapping one another on the back.

Laura always complained that with one parent from Shanghai and one from Kansas City, she should have been a great Eurasian beauty. Instead she was tall and cheerful and not overly coordinated; on her best days she could just manage "professional" at work, and "coltish" in evening wear.

When she saw Dante waiting for her in the church gardens, she stopped and goggled like a startled marionette, grinning and clutching her straight black bangs in a parody of astonishment. She wore a black leather bomber jacket over blue jeans and a black turtleneck, and her silver Chrysler Tower earrings: one-inch-long replicas of the famous art deco skyscraper. In her hand she held a brown paper bag; bread crumbs for the carp, no doubt. She had Chinese eyes and a Kansas jaw and features more expressive than beautiful. She made one of her granny faces, peering suspiciously at Dante over the tops of her little round glasses. "You're so . . . white!" She pursed wide lips in a worried little frown and peeped at the other families strolling through the gardens. Quite a few of them were mixed, of course, but somehow Dante felt terrifically tall and pale and Hungarian. "What can this fish-faced omen mean?" Laura peered anxiously into her paper bag as if consulting an oracle, and then tossed Dante a bread crumb with a nervous granny toss.

"Studying the natives," he said. Usually it was the easiest thing in the world for Dante to joke with her, but today it took all his savoir-faire to stand in the garden of Twelve Dreams Episcopal Church like a solemn balding red-haired fish.

Laura laughed. "So what brings you here, heathen? Scanning the crowds of churchgoers for likely Break and Enter suspects?" Her quick eyes darted to Jet, still sitting on the bench beside the water. "Hi, Jet! It's been a long time."

"Just felt like seeing you," Dante said awkwardly.

"Too much family to bear for a whole long weekend, eh?"

Dante laughed nervously. "Yeah, I guess. Can't get rid

of them," he added, nodding over at the bench.

Laura grinned, and then looked curiously between the brothers. "Say, Jet, are you an atheist too?"

Jet laughed. "Afraid so."

"How quaint! Dante's the only one I know my own age. Usually they're all old, you know. Hard to keep your unbeliefs, since the War."

"My father's doing," Dante explained. "It's some kind of ethical thing."

"Sarah is straying," Jet commented. "I catch her touching her cameo for luck sometimes. She's shopping around for a good God at a reasonable price."

Dante started, wanting to say, *Are you sure?* But of course Jet would know. He always knew this sort of thing.

While Dante never did.

Jet grinned. "But Dante and myself soldier on, the last acolytes of a dying non-faith."

Laura grinned back. "So have you come to smash the temple, or do you just want a chance to preach before the un-unbelievers?"

"Neither," Jet said. "Actually, Dante needs your help."

Laura frowned. "Is this another girlfriend I'm supposed to tell about a Mysterious Ailment?" she demanded. "Because if so, you can forget it. I'm not doing that kind of garbage again, at least not until you get a more convincing cover story. I finally told her you'd become traumatically impotent, you know."

"Impotent!"

"Actually," Jet said, stepping in smoothly, "Dante needs someone who speaks Chinese."

Laura blinked, dipping into her paper bag and tossing

a handful of crumbs into the clay-colored pond. "Why?"

"Angels."

"Oh ho!" Laura quirked an eyebrow and looked at Dante with new interest. "I didn't think you were ever going to take the plunge."

"I was pushed," Dante said morosely.

She looked at him with sudden concern. "Oh, hey. When was the last time you saw a doctor?"

"Why? Do I look sick?"

"Um, no; it's just that the angel the cops brought in asked about it. She thought maybe you were going in for surgery or something. . . ." Laura trailed off, seeing Dante blanch.

The brothers exchanged a long look. Then Jet laughed.

The bastard, Dante thought. All right. "Look, Laura, there's something I've got to say, before we go any further." He reached out and took her hands in his own. Ideally, the woman you love melts into your arms at this point, eager to hear your declaration.

Laura froze, wary and unsmiling.

Dante's heart flinched, feeling her recoil, and his color deepened. Christ, you're already dying, he told himself savagely. Show a little poise. "Listen, Laura, it's really hard to explain, but I think I'm going to die soon—really soon—and I just had to tell you that I love you. I've loved you for a long time, only I was too stupid to know it. I know it doesn't really matter now, only I had to say it. And I'm sorry."

Lily pads shook and shuddered in the water. Bits of floating bread vanished, one by one, beneath the surface of the pond, jerked down as if by invisible hands.

"Die?" Angrily Laura pulled away from him. "What

the hell do you mean by that?"

"Die. Cease. Halt. Expire," Jet said helpfully. "Perish. Pass away."

"It's—it's kind of hard to explain," Dante stammered.

"Then don't!" Laura shouted, turning and stalking away. "God, if this is some kind of mournful suicide bullshit, I hope you don't expect any fucking sympathy."

"Ebb. Terminate." Jet studied the pond. "I believe my line is, 'I told you so.' "

"Shut up." Dante hurried after Laura. "No, look, it's not suicide," he said, pleading to the back of her leather jacket. "It's more like a, a medical thing. A cancer."

"Of all the cheap ways to try to get laid, this is the cheapest," she snapped, striding down the narrow gravel path as if it were paved with Dante's face: crunch crunch crunch. "I can't believe you think this is actually going to work on me. I know your lines, you piece of shit. If I wanted to decorate in used condoms, I could do the Empire State Building with what you throw in the trash."

"That's not fair," Dante said angrily, grabbing her by the shoulder. "This is me, Dante. You know I'd never try to pick you up."

(Jet winced. Oh, great going, D. *There's* a line calculated to win a woman's friendship.)

"Don't touch me," Laura spat, spinning and knocking Dante's arm away so hard it went numb from the elbow down.

Belatedly Dante remembered that Laura went to some sort of martial arts class.

It was his right arm too—the one with the bandaged hand at the end of it from where he'd grabbed the lure. Ow, ow, ow: feeling flooded back into it.

This was not an improvement.

They stood glaring at one another. Tactful Chinese couples flowed around them like water splitting around a rock. "I think you broke my arm," Dante muttered.

"Don't be a crybaby."

They glared some more.

"I mean Christ, Dante. What am I supposed to do with this?" Laura said at last, turning and walking on. "Swoon? Fall into your arms and confess my hidden passion?"

"Get a splint?" Dante suggested, managing a weak grin.

Laura bit her lips to kill a smile. "This hurt?" she said, squeezing Dante's forearm.

Dante squeaked. "Some," he gasped.

"Crybaby." Laura stood still, looking out over the carp pool with her fists jammed into the pockets of her bomber jacket. "Christ, Dante, you hardly even know me."

"I guess having tea every day hardly counts, eh?"

"Telling a girl stories about screwing other girls does not count as knowing a woman's heart, no."

"That's not fair."

"Isn't it?" Laura said sharply. "I wonder. Tell me, where am I going now, hey?"

Dante blinked. "Um, I don't know. Home, I guess."

"Where do I go every Sunday after church?"

"Every Sunday? I, um . . ."

"Every Sunday," Laura said bitterly. "Yeah, every fucking Sunday after church. Where do I go, hey? Where?"

Dante stared at her helplessly.

"Where, damn it!"

She turned from him, disgusted.

"I told you, I don't know," Dante said softly. "I wish I did, but I don't. I wish I could make up for a lot of things, but there just isn't time—"

"Don't tell me that," Laura said warningly.

"There isn't any time anymore. Jesus, Laura. I'm not . . . I don't want anything from you. I don't expect that. I just wanted to say what was on my mind, that's all."

"It's a pretty cheap indulgence. Why the hell tell me? Why not just go ahead and die, damn it, and send me an invite to the funeral? Why do this?"

Dante sighed. "That was Jet's advice."

"You should have listened to him."

If I hear that much more often, Dante thought, I'm going to get angry. "Okay, so I made a jackass of myself and ruined your day, but hell, I'm the guy with four days to live. I think I'm entitled to a little resentment too."

Laura glowered at him for a long moment. "Not to mention fear, anger, denial, and bargaining."

They giggled.

"Oh God, don't laugh, it's too horrible," Laura whispered. "God. How can I make jokes?"

"My mother would say it's the only possible response."

"Yeah, well, I bet she's not laughing now."

"Haven't told her yet." Dante reached out to take Laura's hand. His bruised arm screamed and he thought better of it. "Take me with you," he said.

"What?"

"This is Bargaining," Dante said rapidly. "It comes after Denial and before Acceptance. Take me wherever you go every Sunday after church." *Four and a half days.* I know, I know, god damn it. But this is one of those things I'm supposed to settle up, isn't it?

"I thought you needed my help for some angel thing. Speaking Chinese."

Jet had caught up with them. "And being Chen Dai Fei's great-niece," he added.

Dante shook his head impatiently. "That can all wait. Take me with you, now."

Laura shook her head in disbelief, sending the Chrysler Towers crazily spinning. A couple of tears ran down her cheeks and she wiped them angrily away. "This is not one of your smoother pickups, you bastard."

Dante had never seen her cry before. "Hey," he said softly. "It worked, didn't it?"

They were going to visit Laura's mother.

" 'A house is a machine for living in.' Le Corbusier said that." Laura maneuvered her Elegant Vehicles compact through the narrow streets of Chinatown, angling for Main. Dante sat in the passenger seat, surreptitiously rubbing his bruised right arm. Jet was tactfully absent; he would meet them later, back at Dante's apartment.

Laura waved at the office towers rising around them as they cut through downtown. "Machines for living in. Ghastly, isn't it? Chen Dai Fei used to say, 'A building is a harlot's gown—' It emphasizes the positive and hides the flaws. You know the old saying, the woman should wear the dress, not the dress wear the woman? That's the idea with architecture too. The house must make its occupants feel beautiful, serene. It's all a question of priorities: do you shape the people to fit the machines, or the machines to fit the people?" The Chrysler building swirled, an art deco teardrop hanging beside her cheek, as she glanced over at him. "Get it?"

"Uh, I think so."

"My great-uncle was the one who came up with the big symbol—tearing down the Wall and using its stones to pave the Permitted City's East Gate and the Winding Road. That's why Dad was in the first wave of urban planners to be sent out into the world."

Dante frowned. "Why did he want to leave a perfect city?"

"He didn't." Laura shrugged. "But China needed exports, needed to show off her talents, and really, really needed hard Western currency. Uncle Chen ordered Dad to go, and like a dutiful nephew, he went. That was 1961. The Permitted City had been up and running for three years—long enough to produce the numbers the Mandarinate needed to prove the idea to the rest of the world. Production stats, crime stats. Icing on the cake, really. All they had to do was take any visitors through; let 'em live in the place for a week or two. Meet the people. Walk in the Gardens." She shrugged. "It ate my father away, you know. Coming here. After all that work, to leave the perfect city and have to live with this." She gestured at the motley collection of skyscrapers and boutiques, blues pubs and porn shops around them.

"Like being tossed out of Eden."

"Yeah." Laura laughed. "Of course the Americans were damned if the slants were going to make a Perfect City before them! This was Kennedy and Johnson and the Great Society, remember. But as soon as they tried to build a perfect city of their own, they slapped it down on a grid that would have made Corb proud. The Elegant

Prison model, as my father used to say. Just like Henry
Ford's factories: the great American method was to make
the humans adapt to the convenience of the machines.

"The Permitted City proved how much more produc-
tive a happy worker is. Before that, only left-liberal so-
ciologists were interested in whether treating people like
ball bearings was such a good idea. But magic caught
Americans by surprise, see. They were the greatest empire
of the Rationalist Age and they just couldn't use their
angels right. In China, they'd been using feng shui to help
design houses and gardens for thousands of years. They
had a nice, clearly defined social use for magicians already in place; and the higher the magic rose, the better
use they made of them."

"That's why it's good that you speak Chinese," Dante
said, scrambling to put things together.

Laura nodded. "And even better that I'm related to one
of the Permitted City's inner circle. Things Chinese are
very hot in angel circles." She glanced at Dante again.
"It's not that Chinese angels are more powerful than angels anywhere else. They're just less marginalized. They
actually have a place in society, a role to perform."

"Rather than pissing their lives away without direction," Dante said dryly.

Laura shrugged. "Your words, not mine."

But that was it, of course. That was another reason he
had never tried to date Laura. It wasn't just that he was
afraid of intimacy; it was that he knew she wouldn't be
interested. That was the bitter truth of it, Dante told himself. As a friend, old Dante could be pretty entertaining.
But as a husband, a man with his shit together on whom
you could depend?

A man you'd trust to raise your children?

Get serious. Laura would never dream of pinning herself to a man with the direction of a butterfly.

The thought made him close his eyes in self-disgust. Never had the gulf between them seemed greater.

Laura was a professional woman with a vision of her future and something to contribute to her community. While the only thing I have left to contribute, Dante thought bitterly, is a seven-pound sack of white silk feasting on my internal organs.

Laura turned onto a gravel drive that led into a small park on the side of a hill dotted with evergreens; all as serene and lovely as a cemetery. Dante had never seen Laura's face so controlled and expressionless. "Welcome to Seven Cedars Nursing Home," she said. "Mother's inside."

"A retirement home is an interesting challenge for an architect," Laura remarked as she signed herself in at the front desk. " 'Flowing space' is all very well, but here you can't use changes in level to separate one area from the next." Dante's eyebrows rose. "Broken hips," she said tersely. "Any steps or ramps would make this into a machine for dying in. More than it is already, that is."

From the front desk area (a pleasant atrium welling with natural light) she led him along a wide, winding central corridor. "This is one technique," she said. "Rooms come off a central artery; the artery widens into a common area, then curves. Makes for a winding building, but each little set of suites feels more private, without having to introduce heavy doors or dangerous steps."

She stopped and tapped her foot on the floor. "Custom

carpet." It was a strange design, now that Dante came to look at it: two rich brown strips on the outside, and a wide golden band down the middle. "Carpet is better than tile for cushioning falls, obviously, but it has to be very flat, to make walking as easy as possible. The color scheme has to maximize contrast for people whose eyesight is failing: by following the gold band they can avoid walking into the walls. The wrong level of contrast will make them scared: a really dark band in the middle makes them feel they're walking in a trench; something too light, and they think they're balancing on a curb."

An old woman trotted by them as if jogging an endless marathon. She was thin, terribly thin, and *frayed*, Dante thought.

(He remembered the same look on his grandmother's face as she lay in her dim room under the big bedspread, the one with huge poppies sewn in riots all over it. The room had smelled of dust and hairspray. She had smelled different too: not like garlic and paprika and port anymore, but like pee and used-up flowers. She never really looked at him, standing by her bed, but her thin old fingers played with his shirt cuff, rubbing it, tugging it, sliding the cloth back and forth across her fingers until he ran from her like a witch in a fairy tale, ran outside and down to the river, where he sat swinging his legs over the end of the dock and crying.

Jet had stayed. Dante had been too scared, but Jet had stayed to the very last moment, to the mysterious instant when the candles went out and the last wisp of smoke coiled up to the ceiling.)

The old woman in the retirement home was mumbling as she hurried by. Her right hand plucked repeatedly at the collar of her blouse, a mindless, mechanical motion she didn't seem to notice. Dante shuddered. "Why do they do that?"

"Trying to feel," Laura said. "Sense of touch goes too. Didn't you know that? That's Mrs. Clithe. She can't feel the edges of her silverware anymore, can't remember what the spoon is for, or the fork or knife. The staff do what they can, but she doesn't eat much these days. Just runs through the corridors. Goes through three pairs of sneakers a year, they say."

"Jesus." Dante looked at Laura. Her face was still set and expressionless.

Glancing through an open doorway into one of the suites, Dante saw an old man lying in bed, and heard voices coming from an unseen TV. A pair of Velcro straps ran over the man's body, like seat belts in a car.

"That's Mr. Silverstein. He used to be an absconder," Laura commented. "Staff spent half their time combing the grounds for him."

"Is that why they locked him up?"

She shook her head. "They get paid to chase him. But he's lost too much now: he's violent most of the time. It's 1944 for him. He's not sure where he is, but he knows they've got him imprisoned here. The staff are the Nazis who gassed the rest of his family. He's waiting for them to torture him."

"Paranoid."

Laura pursed her lips. "It's the best and most logical theory he could devise, Dante. How else to explain why a twenty-four-year-old Jew from Warsaw is being strapped to a bed in a house where everyone else is old and feeble and useless?"

Time like a sequence of slides, Dante thought. But there are only a few slides left, and a pile of shattered glass. How to build a life around a few moments and a few facts? How to resurrect a man from his thumb bone and a faded photograph?

"This is why you live in my building, isn't it?" Dante said quietly. His glance took in the custom carpet and the beautiful grounds, visible through wide windows in each common area. Across the way a long-suffering nurse helped an old man into his bathroom. "This is where your money goes."

Laura didn't look at him. "My mother's suite is just ahead."

Sally Chen was sitting at a polished cherrywood table overspread with a white lace cloth. A photo album lay open in front of her, and she was picking at the plastic film over one of the pages. Finally she managed to peel it back with a sticky, tearing sound. Then she pulled out one of the pictures on the album page and put it in a small pile beside her. There might have been a dozen snapshots already in the pile.

Laura's mother was from Kansas. She had moved to the big city and met Chen Shoyu while working as a secretary in the architecture firm he joined as a high-priced consultant. Time had come like a prairie wind and stripped the big city from her, leaving her weathered and raw-boned and gaunt. Dante thought, *She doesn't eat much anymore.*

"Hi, Mom. It's me. Laura."

The old woman looked up, seeing them for the first time. She blinked, as if trying to collect her thoughts.

Distractedly she smiled. "I have a daughter named Laura; isn't that funny?"

Laura's long face was expressionless.

Mrs. Chen cocked her head to one side, and ran one big-boned hand through her thin gray hair. "You remind me of someone," she murmured. "Oh, of course," she said, embarrassed. "You're Bill's new wife. How silly of me."

"No, that's Aunt Cindy." As her mother's smile faded, Laura walked briskly over to the table. "This is my friend Dante," she said. "So what are you doing today?"

Sally Chen turned back to the photo album with obvious relief. "Looking at pictures. I don't have much to do here, but I do like my pictures. Only someone else has gotten their pictures mixed up with mine, so I'm trying to set things in order." She looked over at Dante, making an effort to include him in the conversation. "I get such a comfort from them; I hate to think of someone else missing their photos!"

Her voice faltered, and her eyes became distant. She was still looking at Dante, but he could tell she wasn't really seeing him. Talking was an effort for her, something she did because she felt it was proper; but most of her energy was directed elsewhere. To listening, Dante thought suddenly; listening to something deep inside herself. Pain. Pain and the whisper of blood, and aching joints, and the whole rot of her insides. Listening to her own decay.

He thought of the white sac growing slowly inside himself. What if he had to listen to that cancer growing there for years? Wouldn't he have this same distracted air? Would he even do as much as Laura's mother did? Or would he hunker down, unable to think of anything but his own corrosion?

"It's the staff's fault," the old woman muttered. "They're always misplacing things. Stealing things too," she added bitterly. "And they won't take messages. They never take Shoyu's messages for me. I go down to the desk three or four times a day and listen, just listen to them answer the phone, but they're very clever."

Gently Laura fanned out the photos her mother had winnowed from the family album. The pile of discards were all of Laura: Laura at thirteen in a ponytail and shorts, blowing out birthday candles. Laura graduating from high school and University and architecture school. Any Laura more than six or seven years old. "I'm sure they do their best," she said gently.

Her mother bit her lip. "What's he going to do?" she whispered. "He doesn't know what to put in her lunch. He said she should just eat at the cafeteria, the idiot. Doesn't understand what it means to be a cafeteria girl. The other kids will tease her. They'll tell her that her mother doesn't love her."

"She'll be fine," Laura said gently.

Laura's father had died in '85. They had flown his ashes back to China.

"What will she think?" Sally Chen said tearfully. "Why doesn't her mommy come home anymore? She's six years old!" Tears ran from her eyes; she covered them with a gaunt, long-fingered hand. "Why doesn't her mommy call? She thinks I don't love her. She's forgotten me."

"She hasn't forgotten you."

"Every night I pray to God and I ask, How long do I have to stay here? How long, sweet Jesus? How long?"

Laura cradled her mother's gray head in her arms.

She lived in a little flat in a poor section of town so her mother could be cared for. And once a week (or twice, or five times, for all Dante knew) she came here and endured this.

Why?

Dante looked with angel's eyes, and felt understanding break open inside him (where blood ran whispering through veins long left dry).

This place made Laura strong. Not her job or her professional degree, but this. Her mother's head, cradled in her arms, had forced her to leave her own childhood behind as Dante never had.

How insubstantial he must seem to her. Laura, who faced this every week; how could she help but despise a man who could not face himself?

In time the crying stopped, and Sally Chen's old hands reached once more for her family album. Two heads bent over the pictures, murmuring: one glossy black, one iron-gray.

Near the end of the book, the page fell open to a picture of Laura's mother, taken only two or three years earlier, when she was still living in the family house. She balked, picking at the plastic film, frowning at this stranger. She doesn't recognize herself, Dante thought. In her mind she's still thirty-four, with a young daughter, thanking God and her stars for the new life she's found. She looks in the mirror of the family album and doesn't recognize the face looking back.

What mystery moved her, then, to scrabble suddenly

at the album, and pull the picture out, and tear it into pieces before Laura could react? Tear it and tear it into scraps of color, her hollow cheeks flushed with outrage. Her rasping breath harsh.

"She's not a monster," Laura said as they were leaving.

"What?"

"I saw the way you looked at her. She's not a monster. She's not grotesque." Laura's dark eyes were bleak. "She's an old woman going senile. It's a fact of life. It will happen to me."

"Not necessarily," Dante said. "Even with genes and whatever, there's a long time between now and . . ."

Laura unlocked his door and walked around to the other side of the Elegant Vehicle. She had painted a pair of eyes on the front side panels, to help see accidents coming. "You've got to check these things before proposing," she said, smiling humorlessly. "Like inspecting a used car for rust before you buy."

She opened her door and slid inside. "At home I've got three feathers in a bowl on top of my votary."

"I remember," Dante said, seeing again her beautiful apartment, all cherrywood and brass, the three feathers in the bowl, arranged like flowers, almost but not quite breaking the subtle harmony Laura had fashioned there.

"They're from a hawk my mother shot when she was fourteen years old. It was a red-tailed hawk; they thought it might have taken one of their chickens. Used to hang around the farm. So anyway, one day my mom shot it. Took it down against a clear sky with her own .22. I asked her why she kept the feathers, you see. That's how I know the story." Laura's face, so full of expressions, was empty now. "She grew up in this little Midwest town. She stole books from the library because the librarians wouldn't let her take out anything that wasn't from the children's section. It was hot in the summer and the dust blew in her throat and sometimes she felt like she was suffocating standing up, just standing up.

". . . I asked her why she shot the bird. You know what she said? '—Because it was free.' "

Delicately, Dante touched the thread of Laura's guilt. On angel's feet he followed it into her darkness. "In China she'd still be at home, wouldn't she?" he said softly.

"This isn't China," Laura said, twisting her key in the ignition.

Fierce as a hawk.

CHAPTER
TEN

SUNDAY DINNER WAS QUIET WITHOUT DANTE AND
Jet. When the meal was over and the dishes had
been done, Sarah absently closed the fridge door a
small hand had pulled open. A moment later she whirled,
heart in her mouth, only to find she was once again
alone. And yet, there on the floor she clearly saw a set
of muddy sneaker prints, about the right size for an eight-
year-old child, trailing from the refrigerator to the
kitchen door.

The sight raced over her like frost, making her skin
tingle, then go numb. Still and cold she stood, like a little
girl turned to glass; that empty and breakable.

With sudden clarity she saw that a kind of fairy tale
was growing up around her. Dante and the other angels

were only seeing the beginning. It was a new world now, the world of her grandmother's Hungarian fairy tales: a world of witches, of talking beasts and crying statues, of omens and wolves and wicked stepmothers. Like a little girl lost, she stood in the kitchen, enchanted into glass. The magic Dante dreaded so much was hissing down around her like the rain, blurring her view of her parents' fine rational world, tickering against her glass arms and legs, creeping down her glass cheeks; and the night rose up and up, running like a river in her heart.

O God, her little girl.

She forced herself to move.

It shattered her inside. Her little girl.

Splinters of grief exploded in her chest. She couldn't bear it. How could she bear it? She couldn't, not without help. She had always prided herself on her toughness, but since Dante found the body in his bedroom something had made her weak, had shown her how fragile her life really was, and then come to blow it all apart.

She looked wildly for Aunt Sophie. On the main floor, in the basement; she ran upstairs and banged on Sophie's door without getting an answer. Ran back into the parlor. Something—a faint creak from the back porch, a sound like a small body leaning against the screen—drew her to the kitchen door. She peered down to the boathouse and saw Aunt Sophie standing on the dock.

It was cold dusk outside. She ran down through the garden and out to the end of the dock, her feet suddenly loud on the planking. There she found Aunt Sophie, swaddled in her big wool coat, looking into the river.

Sarah was breathing hard, sending clouds of gray vapor into the chilly air. "I've got to talk to you."

Aunt Sophie did not even turn.

"I've got to talk," Sarah repeated. She was crying. "I have to talk to someone and you're the only one who can understand."

Up behind the house the tallest maples raised their bare branches against a pale skyline, but down in the valley it was already dark. The river slid downstream, wide and silent before them, whispering to the wooden dock supports and the patient bank. In the middle of the channel, Three Hawk Island lay like a giant sleeping on his back. A crow flapped heavily across the narrow band of blue sky guttering overhead. Like smoke, he vanished into the tangled darkness of the southern shore.

Aunt Sophie stirred at last; planks squeaked beneath her sneakers. She had a scarf wound around her head, old baba style, to keep out the cold. A cigarette butt shook between her fingers. She tossed it in the river. "Damn birds," she muttered.

"I know about Pendleton," Sarah said. "And Jet."

"You do, do you?" Aunt Sophie watched the river. "That's more than I can say."

"Aren't your hands cold?" Sarah asked. "Put them in your pockets, why don't you?"

Aunt Sophie did not put her hands in her pockets.

"You're crying," Aunt Sophie said. Reaching inside her coat, she pulled out a pack of cigarettes, pausing to accommodate a wrenching smoker's cough. She rummaged in the pack and drew one out. Her old, fat, liver-spotted hands were shaking. She put the cigarette in her mouth and struck a match. It hissed and spat sparks. "All right," Aunt Sophie said. "Talk."

It was the cigarette Sarah remembered: the bitter smell

of it; Aunt Sophie coughing; the red tip wavering in the gloom, brighter and brighter as darkness fell around them. She couldn't remember Aunt Sophie's face at all; her coughs and grunts and terse, bitter swearing came out of the shadows of her scarf, and the cigarette tip danced, glowing, dipping, fainting and fading like a firefly winking above the impenetrable river.

"I was nineteen," Sarah said. "I must have been a slow developer, because it took me that long to be a stupid adolescent. Having left it so late, I really had to work to cram it in."

"I remember." Aunt Sophie coughed—wryly, if such a thing were possible. "Lawrence, wasn't it?"

"It was," Sarah said. "God knows why I went out with it. Its attractions elude me now." (The cigarette tip jiggled, accompanied by a phlegmy chuckle.) "Mostly it was the only thing that showed any interest in going to bed with an overweight social disaster just smart enough to be feared. So I and it went to bed."

"This was before or after your father told him never to see you again?"

"Oh, after. Definitely after."

"Hunh! I told Anton that was a stupid thing to do."

Sarah paused, surprised. So they had talked about her, had they? Well of course they had. Where did this curious blindness come from in children, that assumes parents don't exist except when they're in front of you? Of course they would have argued about her: Mom and Aunt Sophie while cooking dinner, Mom and Dad in bed. Dad and Aunt Sophie at any mutually convenient time; they had bickered continually back in those days.

Still night fell around Sarah like the rain. "So we went

to bed," Sarah said. All the muscles in her stomach knotted up. "I got pregnant."

"Assholes have strong sperm," Aunt Sophie remarked. "You can be safe with a decent guy for years, but a real bastard'll knock you up in no time."

"Of course the first thing I did was break up with him."

"It."

"It. Lawrence. Whether I kept the baby or not, I sure as hell wasn't going to . . . Anyway, Lawrence was out. I didn't know if I would keep the baby. It was paralyzing. For two weeks I walked around like a zombie. I actually got as far as Mom's door once, but I couldn't face going in."

"Ever tell her?"

"Later," Sarah whispered. She closed her eyes. "I walked around in a daze all day. At night I prayed for the baby to die." In her heart, castles were burning.

"—I prayed for it to die. And it did."

For a long second the cigarette tip held perfectly still, red as Mars, a single point of light against the great sliding darkness of the river and the shadowed valley.

Aunt Sophie sighed.

The wooden dock creaked as Sarah rocked back and forth. "I was six weeks pregnant when I miscarried. Six weeks and two days. The pain was incredible. I took a fistful of Tylenol Threes from Dad's bag but I couldn't stop crying. Mom found me in the bathtub in the middle of the night," she whispered. "Sitting crying in the bathtub with blood all over my skirt."

"Sweet Jesus." Aunt Sophie turned, and took one of

the girl's hands in her own. "Shhh, Sarah. You didn't do anything, sweetheart."

"I killed my daughter." Sarah crushed her eyes closed, as if that would somehow stop her from crying. "I wanted her to die and she died."

The river ran, and the old dock creaked sadly in the falling dark. Sarah looked out into the darkness, watching it fill the river valley and spill over its sides, watching the blue sky turn the color of a crow's wing.

"She would have been eight years old," she said.

And Sophie coughed and cursed. "It's not your fault," she said, shaking Sarah angrily. "It happens all the time. It's not your damn fault, okay?"

"Isn't it my fault? How do you know? The mind and the body are hooked up pretty tightly. That's what Dad says."

Aunt Sophie grunted and spat. "Good God, Sarah. Don't listen to your father, of all people."

Sarah opened her eyes to glare fiercely at the darkness. "If it isn't my fault, *why is she back?*" She spun to face Aunt Sophie squarely. "Don't give me the usual line of crap, okay? I came to you because you know what it means to lose a child. Because you lost Jet. Don't tell me it wasn't my fault; that's no damn good to me. Just tell me how to keep from going crazy, will you? Just tell me how to survive. Because I can't stand it, I can't stand it. I can't stand it even one more time God knows; I'm gonna throw myself in the fucking river if I see her again."

The cigarette tip blazed as Aunt Sophie took a long drag. Sarah could hear the crackle as it burned. Then a long sigh; curls of smoke and vapor in the cold air.

Aunt Sophie took her cigarette between two shaking fingers and tossed it into the river. "I don't know what to tell you," she said.

"Do you ever think of Pendleton? I mean, really think of him, anymore?"

"Yeah. I do sometimes." Very slowly Aunt Sophie spoke, and from a deep place, hidden to Sarah. "Yes I do. Sometimes."

"Don't you ever look at Jet?" Sarah demanded. "Don't you ever look at Jet and say, My God, what have I done? What did I make? How did I ever fuck this up so badly?"

Aunt Sophie didn't answer.

"Well how do you stand it?" Sarah was crying too hard to keep the bitter strength in her voice. It broke and went ragged. "Please tell me how to keep going, Aunt Sophie. Because I've seen my daughter three times in the last three days and I really need to know, god damn it. I really need your help."

For a long time, Aunt Sophie did not answer. "I don't know," she said at last. "I don't know how we stand anything. Just too stupid to know better, I guess."

And Sarah was too weak, too weak and hurt and empty, to keep from getting folded into Aunt Sophie's big arms and held, shuddering and sobbing in the cold night. Too weak to stop Aunt Sophie from turning her around and guiding her up the dock and the garden path, big fat limbs sure and comforting as white bread baking, as the sound of sewing machines in the next room; leading her up to the house whose windows gleamed yellow against the darkness. Too tired to run back under the river. Too tired to do anything but climb the back steps at last, and step into the house.

* * *

Portrait

Here are pictures of the angel Jewel; I dug them up in the newspaper archives. Jewel at twenty-six on someone's arm in the Society column; Jewel at thirty-one, giving her plea-bargained evidence at the securities fraud trial of Liam Stratton, the Persuasive Trader; Jewel at thirty-five, acknowledged queen of the city Angels' Guild, in a color photo Time *would use as part of their cover story on the astonishing angel Tristan Chu, 1975's Man of the Year.*

You can see a vision of Jewel in Gainsborough's "Perdita": a delicate, oval face with a small, set mouth, eyebrows surprisingly coarse, and dark eyes that freeze your marrow. Looking into them is like staring down the barrel of a loaded gun: the threat is that naked.

Even her earliest pictures carry this brooding quality. It's most alarming when she smiles. You can see why Pendleton would have fallen for her; to a moth like him, greedy for power, she must have been a wick of pure fire.

Poor Pendleton. Poor, stupid, god damned coward traitor Pendleton.

I got what he deserved.

The Angels' Guild maintained their offices in a spacious Victorian house that had once belonged to a celebrated poisoner. Back in the seventies a journalist had nicknamed it Hell, because it was the one place you could always find a synod of brooding angels. The name had stuck.

Jet and Laura followed Dante as he climbed the porch steps and then hesitated, standing before the heavy oak door. All his life, Dante had tried hard to ignore the angel in himself, but here, on Hell's doorstep, he found himself wondering if the time for that was past.

Maybe—the thought came with a sudden surge of unexpected longing—maybe he could be proud of what he carried inside himself. Maybe there was a place where he could celebrate his magic, rather than carrying it like one of Jet's unclean secrets.

He shook his head, surprised at himself, and pushed Hell's door open, walking into a long, dim hallway.

From somewhere within the darkness inside, a small bell tinkled, announcing their entry.

Dante hissed sharply between his teeth.

"Looks like a junk shop," Laura said.

Laura liked a certain harmony in her surroundings, but there was nothing harmonious about this place. A collection of coats and scarves and jackets hung from pegs on the wall. Above these ran two long shelves, one on each side, each seemingly cluttered with miscellaneous objects. Aging dolls with cracked porcelain faces, little girls' ice-skates, sleeveless records and derelict turntables, radios with broken vacuum tubes, a twelve-year-old's pretend velvet cocktail dress, and a Mason jar holding an ancient marble collection: the sad remnants of a hundred lives. "Are you sure this is the right address?" she said.

"Oh yes," Dante whispered.

Ghosts swayed and sighed everywhere around him. Each broken toy, each cracked cup leaked its secrets into the dense air. "Can't you feel the memories?" Dante shuddered as the angel in him woke, and began to stir. "It's . . . it's sort of a joke," he finally said. "To you it just looks like junk. But if you're an angel . . ."

With every breath he took in a dizzying perfume of memories, mixed from lust and ancient spite, tenderness and green rage. He wanted to close his eyes, stop his ears, press his arms to his head and hide. "These are magic things," he said, unable to look at the bric-a-brac lining the walls. "Each one is like a dream. Like a dream you can't help having when you walk by."

Surely the whole house couldn't be like this, he told himself. What angel could bear it?

And what could Jewel be like, the angel who founded it? The one he was stupidly trying to find. Jewel hungered for these ghosts, swallowed them whole. Jewel had set up Hell to smolder with memories and old emotions.

He felt Jet next to him, cold and empty as a mirror, camera bumping on his chest like a demon's amulet full of stolen souls. Jet lifted it to take a picture of the hallway. "A joke?" he murmured. "But I don't hear you laughing, D. Where's your sense of humor?"

"On the boathouse floor," Dante said, grimacing. "With a lot of my better parts."

(And he saw Laura's Chrysler Tower earrings spinning, spinning; her long hand, with her mother's talon buried inside, her long hand reaching, reaching for the bottom of a tarnished bird cage on her right, where a pair of black-handled scissors lay, with a twist of long blond hair curling around the blades. The blades were bright, shiny and attractive. Laura reached for them through the open bird cage door.)

"For God's sake, don't touch that!" Dante hissed, grabbing her hand.

Laura jumped back, spooked and angry, her hand cocked and bunched into a fist. For an instant he thought she was going to crack him on his bruised arm again, but she held back. "Come on," he pleaded, and after a moment's stiff resistance she allowed him to pull her down the hallway.

A door opened, revealing a sharp-featured woman dressed in severe silks. "Welcome to Hell," she said, tense and unsmiling. "I'm the virgil tonight."

Jet snickered. "And this is Dante!" he cried, presenting his brother. "He's been looking for you for some—"

"Dante!" The virgil's eyes widened. "Um—wait just a second. Don't go away!"

They heard her footsteps pounding up an unseen flight of stairs.

Jet watched her go. "He's been in need of a Virgil for quite some time," he finished. "Well, D., I'd say they've been expecting you."

"Oh shit," Dante said weakly.

"That was the angel the cops brought in to check out your place," Laura said. "I'm sure of it." She looked at Dante thoughtfully. "She was definitely hiding something that night. Angels do that a lot when they think other angels are involved in a crime; at least, that's what the cop said."

Jet frowned. "You know, if any of the angels in here can regularly predict the future, they may well be expecting us." He shook his head. "Isn't that a curious feeling: that someone else may know what we're going to do, before we know ourselves."

The hallway door opened and the virgil returned, accompanied by a middle-aged Chinese-American man with a narrow, hatched-shaped head. His fingers were dry and light. To Dante everything about him seemed light, as if instead of watery organs and muscles, something altogether more fleeting and electric filled his skin. He reached to shake Dante's hand. At his touch, a humming shock flew up Dante's arm and crackled over his body like sheet lightning.

"Good evening," the stranger said in unaccented English. "My name is Tristan Chu."

In the room behind him, five or six angels sat watching. Dante wondered if any of them knew how this visit would turn out. Not for sure, if Aunt Sophie's coins were any indication of how future-telling usually worked. Not with all the details.

Dante still felt shaky from Chu's touch. In a white sac inside himself he felt something stretch, and blindly move.

He willed it to stillness.

Jet nodded, studying Chu. "You were one of Jewel's pupils. I recognize you from the pictures."

Chu turned to Jet. The pleasant smile he had prepared died in a quick hiss of breath. He reached out, running his fingers lightly over Jet's butterfly birthmark, like a blind man reading Braille. "This is about you," Chu said flatly.

"Don't *touch* me," Jet said, slapping Chu's hand away from his face. There was a quick hiss of indrawn breath from the angels watching in the sitting room.

Chu shuddered, looking at his fingertips. They were red, as if tracing Jet's butterfly had burned them. "My apologies," he murmured. "Terribly rude of me."

Laura had recovered from her initial astonishment. "Tristan Chu! I've always wanted to tell you how much

I love your work! The stadium, of course, but particularly the hospital."

Chu smiled thinly. "It is a quirk of history that the hospital has been overshadowed by that stupid World Series fiasco. But after all, home field advantage existed long before Harmony Stadium." He shrugged. "I just . . . gave it its head, that's all."

Dante must have looked as confused as he felt; Jet leaned in and murmured, "Remember the '75 Series? The Indians took game seven at home on back-to-back inside-the-park home runs."

"But a hospital where people actually *get well!*" Laura said. "That's Permitted City calibre work."

Dante wasn't sure he'd ever seen Laura in awe before. It made him uneasy. "Laura Chen. Chen Dai Fei's great-niece," he added pointedly.

"Ah," Chu murmured, and he made a little bow. "Please remember me to your revered uncle. It has been"—he frowned—"three years since we last spoke."

Chen Dai Fei had died in 1977. Somehow Laura was sure Tristan Chu knew that very well.

"I'm here to see Jewel," Dante said.

"Ah." Delicately, Chu spread his hands. "Unfortunately, no one has seen her for days. . . . And there is a kind of madness leaking underneath her door." Chu hesitated. "She taught me a great deal, many years ago. Last week I dreamed her very dark; so dark I caught the first plane from Cleveland." He paused to look at Dante once again. "I dreamed that she had gone to Hell . . . and I dreamed that you were there with her."

"Me?" Dante yelped.

Chu shrugged. "A gatekeeper with the devil's eyes,

then, whose shadow wore a butterfly." He turned to Jet. "Tell me, are you an angel or a Sending?"

Dante knew Jet well enough to see the anger behind his twin's upraised eyebrows. He watched Jet raise his camera and shoot Tristan Chu—*Snap!* "Are those my only choices?"

Chu blinked, dazzled by the flash. "Don't do that again," he said quietly.

"You know what I (*Snap!*) think," Jet went on, ignoring him. The flash jumped like lightning, freezing Chu against the backdrop of broken toys and ancient furniture. "I think our (*Snap!*) friend here was the one that broke into Dante's apartment."

Laura's eyes narrowed, suddenly thoughtful. She looked back at Chu, waiting for him to deny it.

Still blinking, he removed a pair of gold-wire glasses and polished them on his raw silk shirt. "I was concerned," he said.

"Now isn't that nice," Jet observed. "Such concern from a former pupil."

"Jewel demanded certain . . . sacrifices from her students," Chu said. He was ignoring Jet now, speaking directly to Dante. "She had something of mine. Something of me, you might almost say." He frowned. "Of course it had no more right to feel betrayed than, say, a vice that one has outgrown; and yet, I always detected a certain bitterness between this . . . gift and myself. It is very important to me that I understand its current disposition."

"You're afraid to go into her room," Dante said slowly. "You think something has happened to her."

Hooray! one part of Dante cried. . . . Well, no use following this lead any further. No point in staying around this spooky old house, either. While we're at it, let's call the cops and bust Chu's ass for break and enter, the supercilious bastard.

Dante had done his best. You couldn't say he hadn't given it the old college try. And after all, if Jet got this far without knowing what happened at his birth, a few more years wouldn't hurt him. . . .

The pain in Dante's abdomen came back, a sharp stitch that brought his breath up short.

"Let's make a deal," he said, wincing around the pain.

"A deal!" Laura cried. "Let him make a deal with the district attorney. He was rooting through your stuff, Dante!"

Summoning up the ghost of his old charm, Dante waved the whole unsightly affair away. "Nothing there worth stealing: you've told me so yourself a hundred times." He shrugged. "He can tell us about Jewel's friend. The Sending who broke Pendleton."

As he said it, Dante realized how much he didn't know about the Sending. Would the thing Jewel had jokingly called Albert still be in his early thirties, or would he be pushing sixty now, with graying hair? Would time have stolen the cold sparkle from his eyes? Would his fingers slip and slide unfeeling, plucking at the cards, losing their edges when he shuffled the pack?

Chu shrugged. "You mean Confidence, the hustler. Her first true Sending. I've heard of him. I don't know where he is now." He paused, his gaze traveling from Dante to Jet and back. "I could find him—if you were to go down to the study in the basement and look behind Jewel's door."

"Maybe you could find him if I were to go over to a telephone and call the police about a break and enter," Jet said pleasantly.

Chu shrugged. "I wouldn't tell you what you wanted to know, at least not until I was sure my very expensive lawyers weren't more expensive than yours." He gave Dante a quick measuring glance. "But I have a hunch you don't have a lot of time to waste."

Dante looked back at his friends. Crisply Laura shook her head.

Jet remained impassive. Waiting, as he had always waited, for Dante to keep his promises.

This time I won't betray him, Dante thought. As God is my witness. "Okay," he said.

Chu nodded. "Good. Of course, you should be warned that Jewel's study is a dangerous place." He waved his hand at the broken dreams disguised as antique rubbish that cluttered the entryway of Hell. "Far subtler and more dangerous than this. But if you don't mind me saying so, I think you have made the right . . . no, the only choice. You have a destiny here."

Jet's eyebrows rose. "You mean a destiny has him."

CHAPTER
ELEVEN

THEY CREPT DOWN A WINDING STAIR WITH A SINGLE
yellow light at the top; it dwindled away above
them as Heaven must have fled the falling Lucifer.
The way was cramped and narrow and the smell of death
waited for Dante at the bottom of it—black dirt, talcum
powder, urine, leaf mold. Candles.

Once Dante stopped and Jet bumped into him. In the
darkness, where no one could see, he grabbed his twin's
hand and squeezed until he felt the blood come back into
his own fingers. When he started forward again, only Jet
and Laura followed him. Tristan Chu and several other
angels stood waiting in the darkness behind them.

At the bottom of the stairs a thin light leaked out from
under Jewel's closed door, flashing and fading. Its trem-

bling edges slid and shifted, inconstant as the waterline of an unquiet sea. Behind the closed door the restless air soughed strangely, swelling and fading. It reminded Dante of the sonorous throb of summer insects, long ago; him and Jet lying heat-drunk in their fort, bedded in the cicadas' tidal song, among the willow fronds.

"Jesus Christ," Laura breathed. "What's going on?"

Dante's lips were very dry. "I guess I'd better open the door," he murmured. The angel in him unfurled its bright wings and opened its terrible eyes. Dante wanted to run away, wanted to drink wine and watch baseball and forget about all of it, forget Jet's loneliness and Sarah's secret grief, forget the body buried in the muddy soil of Three Hawk Island.

It was impossible. He felt his life splitting, tearing like a silk cocoon, ripping open so the bright-winged angel inside him could tumble out.

Jet snickered from the darkness behind him. "Abandon hope, all ye who enter here."

"Fuck you," Dante said, and he pulled the door open.

Tiny wings exploded around Dante like a spray of flower petals. His yell was cut short as something filled his mouth, fluttering. He spat it out, swearing and swinging his arms. They were everywhere: a storm of butterflies bursting from Jewel's study, whirling up around him and into the darkness. Up, up they streamed, shuddering rags of silk, gold and green, cobalt blue and bloody scarlet. Another volley of shouts and swearing as they flooded around the angels waiting on the stairs. (*Damn right*, Dante thought savagely. *I hope the bastards choke on them.*) Then out, he imagined, shooting from the stairwell like a conjurer's silk handkerchief pulled from a black top hat.

Slowly the flood subsided. Butterflies settled like motes of dust over everything in Jewel's room. Butterflies on the bookshelves and on the glass cabinets, butterflies the size of postage stamps on the escritoire. Monsters the size of Dante's hands flapped slowly on Jewel's desk. Tiny ones, gross ones, lace-edged beauties that crept on thin legs: with each step Dante took they rose like dust from an ancient carpet. They covered every surface, blind and heaving, their frail wings flapping: each of them marked in a curious diamondback pattern.

Jewel was gone, blown into butterflies. She had left her empty clothes behind. Butterflies clambered inside the pair of women's pumps beneath her desk; they struggled, trapped and thrashing, in the limp nylons tangled on the floor. Butterflies crawled on the hem of the businesswoman's skirt lying crumpled in the chair behind the desk. Their unseen wings heaved inside the white blouse lying over the chair's back. The empty silk shook as if it still clothed a beating heart.

Stunned by the madness of butterflies, Dante realized he would never leave the study the same person he came in. Dark things lay in tangles everywhere, memories of naked emotion, sticky as spider-silk, enwrapping him. He could feel them tearing, like tissue, each time he moved.

He stood stock-still, examining the room. Across from Dante sat Jewel's desk, a solid Victorian edifice of oiled brown wood and drawers of the sort that locked with long iron keys. Tall bookshelves loomed over him, with curious trophies on the top. One might have been a mask, hairy-browed and round-eyed, alternately hidden and half-revealed in the pulse of butterfly wings. He saw the skin of a tropical bird; its jeweled feathers trailed from the highest shelf, dimmed with dust. Glass cabinets with bandy legs stocked row after row of liquor decanters, ink bottles, yellowing photographs, and dolls most of all: dolls in porcelain and brass, dolls carved from ebony with painted smiles, leather puppets from Indonesia with long thin arms; dolls of girls and boys and monsters, dolls made from cloth and straw and wax, fine or tattered or mutilated to some unknown purpose. Dolls looking out the windows of a grim Victorian dollhouse like the inmates of an asylum.

"It's Tristan Chu," Laura whispered, pointing at one of the larger dolls. It sat on Jewel's desk, an angular little boy with stiff black hair and glass eyes in a china face.

No, it didn't exactly sit, Dante realized, looking more closely. Only arms and a head extended from the doll's torso. Its legs had been carefully removed. Dante spotted them high on a shelf behind Jewel's chair.

Invisibly and with great deliberation a hidden clock ticked off the slow seconds. Tick. Tock. Tick. Tock. Time heaved and gasped, like wet insect wings.

Behind the desk, Jewel's gray wool skirt and white silk blouse billowed, seething with butterflies. Stirred by paper wings, the air whispered. *O God*, it wept. *O God, O God, O God.*

Holy, holy, holy.

The doll on the desk suddenly smacked its porcelain hands together, crushing a butterfly between its palms.

Laura yelled. Dante screamed. Jet swore.

One gold tooth showed in a narrow smile as with stiff fingers the doll scraped the crushed butterfly off its hands. "Serves her right," it muttered. It glanced up at Dante. "Give me my legs."

"O Christ."

The doll's head turned and it pointed up at the shelf on the back wall to where its legs rested, each foot ending in a shiny patent leather shoe with a silver buckle on top. "Now. Now before Chu comes back. Give me my legs."

"Sweet Jesus." The butterflies stank of madness, so thick Dante could hardly breathe. He felt his mind heaving and fluttering with the pulse of them.

Unsteadily he backed from the study and fled up the stairs, followed by Jet and Laura. The doll was right, he thought savagely: Jewel got what she deserved. She had tried to unchain the angel within herself, and it had come fluttering out at last. Like a story out of Ovid: the god reaching down, the liquid melting moment; and your life exploded, scattered into thin legs and paper wings.

Up on Hell's main floor, butterflies fluttered onto the antiques, balancing on the arms of abandoned turntables, settling on the golden bird cage.

Tristan Chu stood with his arms outstretched, butterflies heaving in each of his palms. His narrow face was grim. "So passes the greatest angel of her age."

"She asked for it," Dante said fiercely. His whole body was shaking. He swept his arm around the room at the clouds of butterflies crawling on silk panels, tumbling from overstuffed chairs . . . marked on Jet's cheek. " 'Do not ask for what you will wish you had not got.' "

Chu looked curiously at him.

"Seneca," Jet explained. "It's one of Father's favorite maxims."

Chu nodded, then looked questioningly at Dante. "And is it . . . ?"

Dante felt like throwing up. "It isn't going anywhere."

"Ah." Chu drew a small gold-plated derringer from the inside pocket of his silk jacket. "Good."

Jet stepped a little behind Dante. Laura stepped a little ahead of him, feet sliding into an inconspicuous fighting stance. Butterflies settled on her hands and hair.

"Would you excuse me for a moment?" Chu said politely. He turned and padded down the stairs. They heard the flat crack of the derringer and a noise like a dozen dinner plates smashing onto a stone floor.

Moments later Chu emerged from the staircase, straightening the lapels of his superbly tailored jacket.

He cupped his hand gently around a diamondback butterfly panting in his palm. Then, gravely, he walked back into the sitting room. The other angels parted for him as he made his way to a table at the back where a coffeemaker stood. Soon he returned with a saucer of warm water, into which he poured three packets of sugar. He placed the sugar water on one of the shelves in the long entrance corridor. Butterflies settled on the saucer's rim and began to drink.

Dante backed away, knowing he had to get out of the angels' hall, with its odor of old secrets. Laura turned to follow him and they hurried outside.

Jet, though, paused, and raised his camera to take a picture of the feeding insects. "Goodnight, Mother," he said. Gently he blew a butterfly off his lens and screwed the cap back on. "Sweet dreams."

A jerky, scraping noise came from downstairs, as of bits of plate being swept across a stone floor.

Every head whipped around to stare at the dark doorway at the top of the basement stairs.

"I wonder about my brother," Jet said slowly to Tristan Chu. "Sendings were Jewel's talent. Architecture yours, I guess. Yours would be tracking," he said, looking at the angel who had come with the cops to Dante's apartment.

Jet began to nod. "Dante, now: Dante's good with dead things. Ghosts have been springing up all around him, these last few days."

From downstairs, a couple of scrapes. A clink. A clatter.

Softly Jet laughed, thinking about how Dante had drawn forth the body on the dresser, then Pendleton's ghost. Understanding just what Dante's presence might mean to the unquiet spirit stirring in the basement.

The first traces of real fear were blooming in Tristan Chu's eyes.

"He's a Resurrection Man," Jet murmured, looking at Tristan Chu with no sympathy at all. "A Resurrection Man whether he wants to be or not. And lo, the dead rise around him."

"What took you so long?" Laura said impatiently when Jet came trotting down to the car a moment later. "You had some business to do with Chu?"

Jet grunted. "Paying my last respects," he said.

He started to explain, but Dante, lying in the back seat, lost the thread of it. He had thrown every last scrap of strength he had into forcing himself down into Jewel's room. Now, after being furious and terrified and halfway to crazy, he was utterly exhausted, drained beyond words. He felt resistless as a jellyfish, as if the sac inside his abdomen had leached all the nutrients from his bones, leaving him strung together by nothing but cartilage and skin.

He slid into dreaming as Jet and Laura talked quietly in the front. Overhead, street lights waxed and waned like so many ticks of Grandfather Clock.

(He remembered riding at night in a long brown car, an Olds or an Impala—Jet would remember. Thrown by the street lights, shadows would sweep over them, swelling and streaming away. They would be coming home from a movie, or a rare restaurant dinner. Always the two of them in the back seat, him and Jet, their legs so short they could swing out straight without touching the seat in front of them. The vinyl upholstery slick and dry as snakeskin. There was an ashtray on the armrest; the little metal lid squeaked when he pushed it open, and snapped shut when he let it go. Push, squeak, snick; push, squeak, snick. It made Father mad.

Push, squeak, snick.

He could feel his father's anger, pushing out from the front seat like a brooding cloud. He didn't know why he kept on swinging his legs, kept on clicking the ashtray; only kept his head down, and did it, like a boy playing jacks while a thunderstorm bore down on him.)

Dream-ridden, Dante drifted on angel's wings. But a part of him never left Jewel's study. Or rather, Jewel's study was inside him now, like a web within his body. A part of him struggled there still, paper wings beating like a dying heart.

He woke gasping from unquiet visions as Laura's car rolled to a stop in his parents' gravel drive. He felt Jet's hand on his elbow a moment later, helping him out.

He flinched at the touch of the chilly autumn air. God, he was so tired. He wished he could clear his head enough to say something reassuring to Laura, but sleep was a poison in his blood, making it hard to think, hard to talk. He might have promised to see her the next day, but he wasn't sure.

Then they were in the hallway, Jet sure and stealthy, Dante leaning like a drunk against a wall, crushing a felt hat on a nearby peg. Long coats and hats and umbrellas hung around him.

Hat?

His father hadn't worn a hat in years. Dante examined the hat, trying to place it. Oh—Pendleton's, he thought with relief. That explained things. Pendleton's snappy fedora, the one he'd clapped on his head as he left the ritzy hotel room. Funny I didn't notice it before, Dante thought. Could have used it when I was dowsing for Pendleton's past.

Something in Aunt Sophie's black wool coat ground into his hip. Blinking, he reached down into one of her pockets and brought up a handful of stones. Dante gazed stupidly at them. Why would Aunt Sophie have filled her pockets with stones? When he finally looked up, he found Jet watching him, dark eyes narrow and thoughtful.

Dante thought, This means something to him.

But nothing that wasn't sleep had a hold on Dante now. He put the rocks back where he had found them and stumbled up the stairs to bed. His head hit the pillow and he was falling.

*　　*　　*

Tumbling from consciousness to a deep and dreamless place, he passed himself, still trapped in Jewel's study.

The study was bare of butterflies this time. Jewel sat behind her desk, dressed in her white blouse and gray wool skirt. There were three other places to sit in her study: a comfortable brown armchair, a hard oak chair beside the escritoire, and a little pine stool in front of the grim doll's house. Dante started to sit in the armchair—

Murder!

—then stopped as dread wailed through him. His heart hammered and his mouth went dry. Very slowly he stood up again, and slowly he took a seat in the hard oak chair by the escritoire. It was implacable, but at least not webbed with horror. He looked at the sinister brown armchair and shuddered.

It's a test, Jewel said. *I can tell a lot about a person from where he chooses to sit.*

"Whether he's an angel."

Jewel shrugged. *And other things. There are angels who would sit in that chair, knowing what you know.*

"Would you?"

I have my own chair, Jewel said, throned in the highback Victorian monster at her desk. Behind her, a tall bookcase rose high above her shadowed face.

"But if you were someone else. If you were a visitor, and felt all this as a visitor would feel it. Would you sit in the armchair, just to show off, or would you sit where I'm sitting, to project all your will and steel and determination? Or would you perch on the stool and play with the dolls?"

Seriously?

Dante nodded.

Seriously, Jewel said, *I would do anything in my power to keep from ever coming in the door.*

As Dante watched, a pair of jeweled wings, indescribably beautiful, fluttered at her throat. A butterfly crawled out from beneath her blouse. *I am a very deadly angel,* Jewel murmured. A second butterfly followed the first. Then a third tumbled from her graying hair and crawled down her shoulder. *You don't have any children, do you?* she said sharply.

"No," Dante whispered.

Jewel shook her head, and another butterfly fell out. *It's my one rule,* she said firmly. *Risk what you like on your own time, fine, but don't screw around with children's lives. I won't let an angel come down my stairs until I know he doesn't have children, usually; but today I'm so . . .* Her words trailed off; confusion filmed her eyes like cataracts.

"No kids," Dante whispered.

Slowly Jewel nodded, extending her arm. *Then give me your hand,* she murmured. *Give me your hand, and I'll press your fingers onto God.*

Like Jet, Dante thought. Pressing his secrets on me.

But he was too far in to back out now. He was trapped, and running out of time.

He held out his hand.

> WHEN IS DEATH NOT WITHIN OURSELVES?...
> LIVING AND DEAD ARE THE SAME, AND SO ARE
> AWAKE AND ASLEEP, YOUNG AND OLD.
> — HERACLITUS

CHAPTER
TWELVE

PORTRAIT

By some universal law, never formally codified but nonetheless immutable as gravity, every album must contain a picture of a pet.

My pet is a colony of rust. I keep it in a glass jar above the radiator; if properly watered, the heat aids its digestion. I used an old nail as a nurse log and stripped the paper from supermarket twist-ties to make saplings. Once each week I try to feed it something nice, a couple of staples if I'm feeling benevolent; a paper clip, coppery and difficult to digest, if my mood is harsh. On Father's Day I give it a thumbtack, and at Christmas it gets the lid from a tin can; each Thanksgiving I drop in a whole ball of steel wool.

I suppose there's a moral in rust, somewhere. Our bodies decay, attacked from the inside by our own free radicals. Our minds are crumbling too, as the magic rises. I read in the Sunday Times *that the number of schizophrenics in the population has doubled in the last ten years, and is expected to double again in the next five. Rot is spreading out from the hearts of our great cities. We live in a world of slow corrosion, and we are all of us rusting from the inside out.*

There's a moral in just about everything, if you care to look for it. I usually do—perhaps too often. Maybe it's enough to say I like my little colony. Even though it's not alive, it grows: an example to us all! It pleases my humor. And this picture is in color, for once, because rust is such a lovely shade of red.

Early next morning Sarah burst in on Dante with Jet hard on her heels. She flung the curtains wide, flooding Dante's room with pale autumn light.

Dante blinked. "Sis?" Still dreamy and confused, he was reassured by the ordinariness of his room and the day beyond his window.

Fragments of dream scuttled like cockroaches into the dark corners of his mind.

He was glad to be awake.

"This has to stop," Sarah hissed, her face white with strain and sleeplessness.

"It's not all Dante's fault," Jet said. "For once."

"You stay out of this!" Sarah cried. "You just want to find your soul or your father or whatever the hell it is you think you've lost. You don't give a damn what happens to the rest of us."

Dante struggled to sit up in bed. Good grief. He had slept in his clothes for the first time since he was twelve years old. His linen shirt was distressingly wrinkled and one of his cuff links had worked its way free. He rooted in the bedclothes until he found it. "What has to stop?"

"You! Whatever angel thing you're doing that's bringing up these ghosts!"

Dante rubbed his eyes, then ran a hand up over his satanic eyebrows and his balding forehead. "What angel thing is that, exactly?"

Jet cackled. "It seems you're a regular Pandora's box, Dante. Ever since we opened you up on Friday night, all sorts of ghastly things have come flying out."

A jolt of adrenaline washed through Dante's blood like ice water, leaving him painfully awake. "Pendleton's hat," he murmured. Jet looked at him, one black eyebrow quirking. "On a peg downstairs," Dante explained. "I saw it when we came in last night, but I was too tired to think straight. It must be more than thirty years old. Did anyone else see it?"

Jet was already out the door. He returned a few seconds later. "It's there all right. Hanging at the end, an expensive satin-lined fedora that was never there before."

"God. I hope Aunt Sophie doesn't see it," Sarah murmured. "Not on top of his ring."

"I think she already has," Dante murmured. Horror crept through him, remembering the pockets of her black wool coat, heavy with stones.

How close had Aunt Sophie come to walking under the river, to a dark place where her old wounds couldn't hurt her anymore?

That's how Pendleton had gone too, wasn't it? Threw

himself in the river when he saw the diamondback butterfly on Jet's baby cheek and knew that he had lost the soul of his firstborn son in a game of cards.

Sarah dropped heavily onto Dante's bed. "You mean you didn't even know what you were doing with this angel stuff?"

Dante smiled weakly. "Big surprise, hunh?"

"Well, could we get you exorcised or analyzed or dry-cleaned or something? Because I'm being haunted now, and I'm not enjoying it very much."

Oh great, Dante thought. Another way to bring a little extra grief down on his family. "Do you want to talk about it?"

"Not particularly," she said crisply. "What I want is to know what we're supposed to do next."

"There is one other ghost," Dante said carefully, trying to make sense of what was going on inside himself. Memories had been flooding back to him since the autopsy. But now, having taken the fateful step into Jewel's room, he was beginning to feel the future too, growing like a cancer inside the body of the present. "Jewel got inside me last night," he said, looking to Jet. "When we were in her rooms at the angels' club."

"Christ." Jet touched the butterfly on his cheek.

"Maybe I raised her ghost, like when I pulled Pendleton up inside myself. Jewel is inside me now. Not just when I concentrate, but all the time. Inside me like a parasite."

"Or a cyst."

Reluctantly Dante nodded. Maybe it was Jewel crouching in that pulpy white sac inside his abdomen: Jewel like a spider with her brood, waiting to hatch.

*   *   *

Jewel knelt beside him (under his skin, below the muscles of his stomach, inside the secret meat at his core) as together they looked at the doll's house. Gently, very gently, Jewel cracked the house open to show Dante to himself, curled up in the parlor at the foot of Grandfather Clock.

The memory cut into him like a scalpel, slicing cleanly through his skin, sinking in just above his third year.

Tick. Tock. Tick. Carpet smells: dust and ash from ancient cigarettes. The nap rough against his cheek.

Grandfather Clock divides time as well as space. Each tick shaves a second off your life. Tick. And one day, Mother will die. Tock. And Father will die. Tick. Aunt Sophie will die. Tock. Jet will die. Tick.

I will die.

Tock.

I will die.

Tick.

He was three years old. He slapped the carpet, and watched the dust motes dance in a bar of sunshine.

Death filled him up and overflowed him. He couldn't grasp it, only feel it overwhelm him, huge and vaporous and terrible.

Tock.

Three years old, he lay with his head on the carpet, already dying, watching the dust motes drift in the bar of sunshine and fall back into shadow.

Light and darkness.

Drift and fall.

Tick.

* * *

You begin to suspect what you already know. Jewel's fingers tensed, tight as wire around his own. *I'll make an angel of you yet.*

"Could Jewel be the one raising the ghosts?" Sarah asked.

Dante frowned. "I don't think so," he said slowly. "Jewel's specialty was Sendings. It's close, but not the same thing. She would fix on an image, a personality or an archetype maybe, and brood over it until it hatched into life. But those were things that existed in the twilight world."

"In the collective unconscious," Jet suggested.

"Right! Right. But this other thing . . . this raising the ghosts of actual people: I think that's me, somehow. There's some kind of, of field or something."

"The Lazarus Effect," Sarah intoned. "Great. Now we're trapped in an episode of *The Twilight Zone*."

"But what about Pendleton?" Jet said. "What about me?"

"Pendleton lost you to a Sending," Dante muttered, struggling to remember a memory that didn't belong to him. It was like trying to read small print in dim light while wearing glasses in the wrong prescription. "Jewel called him Albert, but his real name was Confidence. Jewel looked at Pendleton, and what she saw there—the hustler, the operator—was the germ of her Sending. But of course Confidence wasn't human: he was quick and sly and ruthless as Pendleton could never be."

Dante looked up, blinking. "He was an operator in the City for a time, but something changed. Last Jewel knew he was selling books out of a little shop on the east side called Bargain Books."

Jet fetched a copy of the Yellow Pages. He gave a queer little laugh. "Bargain Books: Let Us Cut a Deal for You." Jet copied down the address and then slowly closed the book. "Maybe I'll pay him a visit, sometime soon."

Dante felt weak relief wash through him. Almost done, thank God. He had almost done his duty to Jet. Lord, he was so tired. Maybe the growth inside him was stealing all his energy, as a fetus robs nutrients from its mother's body. Steady on, he told himself. It's almost over. "Do you want me along?"

Jet shook his head. "You've done everything I could have asked," he said slowly. "If I had known what it might cost you, I would never have started."

"You did know," Dante snapped impatiently. He remembered the press of his own ribs in his back as they wrestled in the grave on Three Hawk Island. The taste of dirt in his mouth, the taste of his own death. "You knew what was under the blanket, damn it. It's too late to say you're sorry now."

"Maybe." Jet closed his dark eyes. "But I am, Dante. I am sorry."

Dante felt Sarah's hand on his shoulder. "It will be okay," she said, hugging him. She sniffed and smiled. "Sorry I've been such a crybaby. But it will work out, D." She gave his shoulder another squeeze. "It will all be okay, somehow."

"Thanks," he said.

Sarah left, but at a look from Dante, Jet stayed. Dante sat on his bed, pulling on a fresh shirt and looking out his window. The last brittle leaves trembled on the poplars in the back yard. Farther on, the garden lay barren, blasted by an early frost. Farther still, the dark river. He had watched it all his life, running endlessly before his eyes and down the valley, into the shadows and beyond his sight, ending up God knew where. In the ocean, he supposed. Lost in the black immensity of the Atlantic.

"Why are we afraid of death?" he asked.

Jet scratched his jaw. "Seems like a reasonable thing to be afraid of."

"I mean, when you're up high you're afraid of falling. When you see a needle you're afraid of the pain. It's not like that with death though, is it?"

". . . No. I guess it isn't," said Jet. Jet always understood what Dante meant.

"It's not a matter of *consequences*," Dante said, frowning. "It just is. The one certain thing, stuck right in the middle of you, like your heart. The one thing you know. You fear it like, like . . ."

"Like you're supposed to fear God."

Dante nodded. From a lacquered box on his dresser he selected a new pair of cuff links, gold set with chips of polished jade. "It's the one thing," he said at last, watching the river. Smooth and dark, flowing out of sight, down to the ocean at last. "The only thing."

The one thing Dante knew he must do was talk to his father. He put it off—as he always put off everything unpleasant, he thought sourly to himself. In a fit of self-contempt he forced himself downstairs, only to find that Father was out delivering liniment for Jess Belton's rheumatism and a charm for Julie Gregson's little girl. Mother was taking advantage of the Thanksgiving Day sales to round up a good turkey, and Sarah had gone into the city. Only Aunt Sophie was left, puttering about the kitchen making one of her special cakes; the counters were cluttered with eggs and lemons and tubs of sour cream.

Frustrated and relieved at once, Dante slunk back upstairs. A bath: that's what he wanted. To loll in a big warm tub like an eight-year-old again.

Oops, he thought, running the water. Should have phoned the lab and left a message on the answering machine. Sorry—shan't be in again. About to die, don't you know. Cheerio. Oh, well; they'd figure it out soon enough.

Gratefully he lowered himself into the wonderfully hot water. Tense from days of near-panic, his muscles ached and sulked, particularly in his back and shoulders, but as the bath water closed over his chest he felt his whole body sigh with pleasure. He touched himself lightly on the abdomen, like a physician checking for appendicitis. He was almost sure he could feel a bulge.

Dante slid slowly under the water, letting it close over his face, blowing a stream of bubbles through his nose. It was wonderfully relaxing, warm as blood.

Three more days, he thought.

A butterfly tumbled from the hot water tap.

"Christ!" Dante swore, watching it heave and swamp, its crumpling wings quickly sodden. "Jesus, Jewel. Can't you do something less disgusting?"

An angel isn't a power, but a conduit for power. If what's inside you is a rose, you bring the rose forth. If it's a tumor, the tumor grows.

Dante fumbled for the soap. "Your definition makes angels sound a lot like loonies," he observed. "My sister tells a joke about that. 'Remember the Son of Sam?' she says. 'Killed twelve people because he said his dog told him to?—I mean, what kind of stupid reason is that? If your dog tells you to blow someone away with a .45 calibre handgun, what do you say?—BAD DOGGIE!' "

Jewel laughed. *Good joke.*

Making a face, Dante scooped up the dead butterfly on the back of a shampoo bottle. Leaning out of the tub, he shook it off into the toilet.

Jewel said, *Why three days?*

"I made a bargain when we did the autopsy. One week to set things straight."

Made a bargain with whom?

"Just—just a bargain," Dante said, annoyed.

With yourself. You made a bargain with yourself.

"What if I did?"

You're the one who thinks you're going to die. You're the one waiting for it.

"So how did you die?" he asked moodily.

—I don't want to talk about that.

"Was it one of your Sendings? I bet it was. Just couldn't lay off, could you? What was it? A Sending of Nemesis, I bet."

Not a Sending.

Something quite different from Dante shuddered deep within his body.

"You should have let it lie, whatever it was."

Yes.

But free will is for humans, not angels. An angel's

greatness is giving way to Greatness. The greater the angel, the less freedom she has. The more she is constrained by the powers around her.

The light went dim in Jewel's study (deep inside him). No longer sitting composedly behind the desk, Jewel walked nervously around her chamber, running her fingers over the back of a favorite book or touching, lightly, a certain mask, as if searching for the reassurance of familiar things. *A wizard tries to control magic,* she said. *An angel is its channel, its riverbed.* She turned on him. *It's not just human dreams—get it? Not just our fancies, our whimsies. It's real. That's what you figure out,* she murmured. *And—* (with difficulty) *and the things we see there are real.*

"Like the Sendings."

She shook her head. *Only partly. Sendings need us. We find them, we bring them into the light. But there are other things too. . . . Chu never touched them. Aster and her crew never looked. They didn't dare, even when I told them. They couldn't bear to hold their eyes open. But last year for the first time I touched something that could walk into the world of its own accord, and walk back again.*

She shuddered. *You know what you call that, don't you?* she asked, with a small, frightened laugh. Stopping before her desk, she stared at a doll sitting on it, a dark-eyed doll with human hair. The doll stared back with wide, watchful eyes.

Under its gaze, Jewel's lace gloves began to twitch and flutter, dissolving into a mass of gray crawling bodies. *You call that a god.*

*   *   *

Dante caught his father in the study after lunch. "Do you have a minute?"

Sitting at his desk, Dr. Ratkay looked around in surprise. "Well, actually—"

"It's important."

Dr. Ratkay squinted, sighed, nodded. Dante came in.

We do look alike, he thought. When did that happen? If I went and looked through Mom's photo albums, what sort of man would I find standing over my cradle?

Slowly Dr. Ratkay swiveled in his chair to face his son. "Well?"

Dante took a deep breath. " 'Those whom God wishes to destroy, he first makes mad—' I'm going to die, Dad." He cut off his father's protest. "I'm going to die very soon, and I want you to promise you won't cut me open. No autopsy, no embalming, no . . . tampering."

Dr. Ratkay settled back in his chair, looking carefully at his son. He seemed small; much smaller than Dante remembered him. The heavy chair before his desk was too big for him now. Dr. Ratkay fixed himself a pipe, his fingers much slower and more precise than usual, as if the least mistake could cut an organ or sever an artery.

"I interned as a pathologist," he murmured at last. "You knew that, I suppose. Did I ever tell you why I came back here to be a GP instead?"

Dante shook his head, wondering at it for the first time. Why had Anton Ratkay come back, a sharp young medical man with a brand new degree? Why come back to his parents' house, to the sickly smell of his mother's lingering death? (The fat old woman tugging at Dante's sleeves, her stringy white hair; her soft bed a trap, like quicksand.) He remembered Sally Chen in her nursing home, tearing pictures of herself into tiny pieces, squares of color so small they lost all meaning.

"Pathologists are the most terrible hypochondriacs," Dr. Ratkay said ruminatively. "Everything is fatal, you see. There's no such thing as a cold you get over, a mild case of pneumonia, a benign tumour. Every time you examine a patient, the case was terminal. Pathologists live in fear." He sighed. " 'The fear which troubles the life of man from its deepest depths, suffuses all with the blackness of death, and leaves no delight clean and pure.' "

"Virgil?"

"Lucretius." Dr. Ratkay tamped tobacco into his pipe. His fingers were shaking. The skin no longer fit them quite right. It hung around his knuckles, liver-spotted, yellow with age and smoke. "I didn't want to raise my children in a pathologist's world."

"Well, you did your best," Dante observed. "With the skull on your desk and your other cheery lessons. Your World War Two was practically a catechism, Dad: And poverty begat Hitler and Hitler begat the Blitz and the Blitz begat Dresden and Dresden begat Auschwitz and on and on."

Dr. Ratkay blinked. "Was I really like that?"

"Were you like that!" Dante said, laughing and outraged at once. "It was like living with Mengele!"

Dr. Ratkay drew a match from a wooden box and struck it. His fingers were trembling. "I didn't mean it," he said softly. "I didn't mean it that way. It's just . . ." He sucked fire into the bowl of his pipe. Tiny strips of tobacco flared and fell to ash, like German villages ignited in Lancaster raids. "It is important to know those things."

"And what kind of name is Dante, anyway? Couldn't you just buy me a bus ticket to Hell on my eighteenth birthday?"

"We went to visit your Aunt Gloria, I believe," his father said dryly. "A close approximation, as I recall." Dr. Ratkay settled back in his chair, drawing on his pipe. His face seemed thin, the lines between his brows deeper than Dante remembered. Wearier.

Anton sighed. "I started medical school in the decade after the War. A tremendous amount of what we knew, especially about physiology and the treatment of trauma, came from wartime research. They used to put dogs in little wooden houses and then blow them up to study the effects. Did you know that?"

Dante swallowed.

"Hm. My reaction exactly. But in the next few years, while I interned and started my practice here, an even more horrible question came up: what to do with the data from the death camps.

"You mentioned Mengele a moment ago. No doubt you have me to thank for making the name familiar to you. But he did a great deal of, of research on people in the camps. So did the Japanese. They called their subjects 'logs.'" Dr. Ratkay's chair creaked as he leaned forward. "'The limb of one of the logs was dipped in liquid nitrogen and snapped off, with the following effects . . .'"

"Why are you telling me this?"

Anton gestured with his pipe, drawing exclamations of blue smoke on the air. "Because that's what life is, Dante! . . . Along with love and grass and skating in winter and good strong black coffee first thing in the morning." He shook his head. "Nobody told me that." He sucked in a long stream of smoke and did not speak, holding it until it began to trickle from his nostrils. Then with a rush it billowed out, clouding his face. "My parents never talked about the hard things. My brother died of fever and we never mentioned him. Leslie was gunned down in his parachute over Italy, and for us he had ceased to exist before his body touched the ground— It's against the Geneva Convention to shoot a man in a parachute," he added, laughing mirthlessly. "As if we play by the rules. As if we wait for the man to drift down before walking up to shake his hand and lead him to comfortable facilities to wait out the war." He snorted in disgust, and billows rolled through the blue smoke now thick around his head.

"You never talked about Aunt Sophie's baby," Dante said accusingly. "You never talked about Jet."

"Well—no. No, we didn't." Dr. Ratkay coughed, troubled. "And maybe we were wrong about that. Your mother wanted to spare Sophie's feelings, and then there was Jet to consider, after all. Still, maybe that was wrong too. To tell only the happy stories: that isn't life. It isn't true, and you deserve better. You deserve to know."

"A little late now, don't you think?"

Angrily Dr. Ratkay laid his pipe aside. "Oh, that's you all right, always sniping. And yet you come to me, saying you are about to die, and you say, 'Father, Father, you have injured me. You told me that war was evil. You told me death was hard.' "

Dante colored. "I didn't mean—"

Dr. Ratkay coughed, a dry, racking spasm that seemed too violent for his thin chest to contain, his narrow rounded shoulders. When did his hair get so thin? Dante wondered. When had his back begun to curve? When had his eyes begun to cloud with cataracts, and something more? Some careful surgeon's look turned inward at last?

"There is only one antidote for death, Dante. Children. A child, now . . . A child cheats time, you see. A child carries a little bit of You into the future. A little bit of hope, a little bit of memory, a few strands of your DNA." He stared angrily at Dante, his old blue eyes fierce. "Let me hurt you some more, my son. There is no Father in a big white beard to make everything better. When you die you rot, and your life rots with you." He leaned forward to grab Dante by the wrist and pulled him close, so he smelled pipe smoke and lime shaving lotion; so he saw the blue stubble a ghostly shadow on his father's aging skin. "You hurt me!" Dr. Ratkay murmured, trembling. "How dare you tell me you are going to die? What stupid words are these? Because I die too, Dante. You kill me, saying that. Do you understand? I die too."

Fiercely his old fingers gripped Dante's wrist, pulling himself out of the chair, movements slow and brittle, as if he had aged many years since he sat down.

And then, slowly, his fingers softened. "But there: I am an old man," he said softly. "I am tough, and I want to be told the truth." Gently he folded his son into his arms, and Dante stooped, awkwardly tall, smelling his father's neck, his familiar cardigan.

"Well, well," Dr. Ratkay murmured. "Whatever

comes, we will look at it together, heh? We will look at it together."

In this memory he was three years old, walking with his dad. It was winter, and when he jumped off the path he sank in snow over his knees. He struggled to get out, arms and legs packed into his snowsuit like weenies inside so many hot-dog buns. He thrashed through the snow, flippering it aside with his mittened hands and laughing until he toppled over.

—Found himself suddenly cold and spluttering, snow on his eyebrows and sneaking inside the tight hood of the snowsuit as he wiped his nose, sniffling, struggling to gain his feet, flailing about in the treacherous snow.

And then his father leaned over, smiling and enormously strong, and lifted him out of the drift; and he laughed and his father swung him around, the two of them laughing in winter, and their breath steamed up together, his father tireless and the white ground spinning under him. He was so happy he didn't need to breathe, it was better than birthdays it was perfect it was flying and he was safe: he was helpless laughter in his daddy's strong arms.

He was safe he was safe and it was forever.

Later that Monday evening, just after dinner, Dr. Ratkay put down his glass of dry French wine and rose from the table. He had intended to put something on the turntable, a recording of one of Beethoven's late quartets by a Czech ensemble he very much admired.

Instead he wavered, as if his entire attention had been suddenly directed deep, deep within himself. Scarlet bubbles foamed abruptly on his lips, followed by a gush of bright arterial blood. He collapsed.

Under pressure from a malignant tumor, an artery in his lungs had given way. They quickly filled with blood. He never regained consciousness.

> THIS IS THE BITTEREST PAIN AMONG MEN, TO
> HAVE KNOWLEDGE BUT NO POWER.
> — HERODOTUS

CHAPTER
THIRTEEN

THE DAY AFTER ANTON RATKAY DIED, LAURA AND
Aunt Sophie stood side by side at the kitchen
counter in the Ratkay house, making lunch. Laura
was dutifully chopping up an enormous red cabbage.
Now here is something Chinese and Hungarians share,
she reflected: a perverse attraction to cabbage. Idly she
wondered if the Mongols had been responsible for that.

Aunt Sophie was making schnitzel. She was also smoking a cigarette, talking around it or holding it between
two fingers while she dipped each piece of veal into her
special batter. Laura couldn't help watching for the moment that a plume of ash would break from Aunt Sophie's cigarette and sprinkle like pepper into the schnitzel
batter.

Laura hadn't exactly meant it to work out like this. She had come for Dante's sake, taking off from work as soon as Jet phoned with the news that Dr. Ratkay had died the night before. She had even brought charm paper and ink and brushes, in case Dante wanted to burn an offering for his father. But the Dante she found when she arrived was disturbingly different; polite and drawn and terribly distant. It was as if everything warm and human in him had turned wooden and ropy at his father's death.

"Just came to help out," she had said briskly, thinking, This is what they mean when they say someone aged overnight. This sudden hollowness, like an empty house. And she remembered her father in the weeks after his first stroke: that clever laughing man, grim-faced and gaunt, struggling to sign his name, or tie his shoes.

So, instead of comforting Dante, she had somehow ended up in the kitchen, listening to Aunt Sophie talk about her little brother's wedding.

"Gwen's father was calm as anything at the rehearsal, but when it came to actually giving away his daughter . . . ! You could see him leaning on her arm all the way up the aisle. Gwen's mother, though: she was something different. She was an old-fashioned schoolmarm with the soul of a pruning hook. I had her for three grades and she scared the spit out of me." The flesh on the underside of Aunt Sophie's big arms jiggled as she lowered her piece of schnitzel judiciously into the skillet. Boiling lard sizzled and spat. "I was shocked to see her cry all the way through the ceremony. . . . Well, I had quite a bit of wine, you see, and caught the bouquet at the reception." Aunt Sophie snorted. "It made me reckless. So: I got my guts together, marched up and said, 'Why were you crying, Mrs. Jones? My brother will be a perfect husband for your little girl!' "

Aunt Sophie paused, glancing sharply at Laura. Laura had never noticed before how curious a color her eyes were, a dull gleaming gray, like old pewter. She had what Laura's father had called "a heavy look"; Laura felt the weight of it, the long years of fierce laughter and grief and finally patience learned at great cost. "You know what Mrs. Jones said? She said, 'Mothers don't cry at weddings because they're sentimental'—all the time she's looking at Anton and Gwen, dancing together in the middle of the room, happy as bluebirds—'Mothers cry because they know how hard it's going to be.' "

Aunt Sophie looked away. "Mothers cry because they know how hard it's going to be."

Schnitzel sizzled in the skillet. Gwen's voice murmured from her husband's study; she was using the phone in there to arrange the funeral and reception, calling relatives and friends and patients all over the country. In the parlor Grandfather Clock ticked calmly, inexorably on.

There was something about the death of Dante's father that was making time do funny tricks in Laura's head. Earlier she had been struck by the old man that had come like a spirit to live behind Dante's eyes. Now, watching Aunt Sophie take a long drag on her cigarette, she could also see the brassy cocktail waitress Sophie must have been, trading shots with her customers, or laughing and drunk at her little brother's wedding. She would have been the sort of woman who drank Scotch, not gin; who stepped up to the booth at the carnival and won her own damn kewpie doll while her date stood back and grinned.

And yet, all these years later, here she was, in the kitchen making dinner, grieving and going on. With a quick flash of anger Laura thought, Isn't that the story of all human tragedy? The men mooning and wordless and withdrawn in the face of anything they couldn't control, leaving it to the women in the kitchen to make the next meal, and feed the baby, and cry: leaving them to do all the hard living in life. Even Laura's father had given up. He had eased himself into Heaven after only two weeks of struggling against his first stroke, leaving his wife alone to face the years that ate away at her like cancer.

Eyes stinging, Laura stood by Aunt Sophie, shoulder to shoulder, slicing her cabbage into ribbons.

Aunt Sophie coughed violently, then spat into the kitchen sink. "That reminds me. Decided if you're going to marry Dante yet?"

"What?" Laura yelped. "Marry him! Of course not! He hasn't even asked!"

"Not yet, eh?" Aunt Sophie shook her head and snorted.

"Why? Did he say he was going to ask?" Laura's mind went racing back to the previous Sunday when Dante had told her that he loved her.

Aunt Sophie took a long drag on her cigarette. "Didn't say that, exactly."

"Well, what did he say?"

Laura could have sworn there was a glint of amusement in Aunt Sophie's eye. The older woman coughed and waved her hand, pulling a ribbon of smoke through the air. "Oh, nothing. Not to me, anyway."

Laura glared at her.

" 'Course, a woman like you must get plenty of offers," Aunt Sophie continued mildly. "Good job. Nice hair. And if you want a family, you'll be wanting to start soon." Aunt Sophie appeared not to notice the way Laura's almond eyes narrowed. "I mean, you're already older than Gwen was when she had Sarah, and was that a handful! Some people say to wait, you need the money, but myself, I think the energy's more important." Sophie scooped the last pair of schnitzels out of the pan and onto the serving plate.

Laura gritted her teeth. The worst part about this outrageous turn the conversation had taken was that Sophie was saying just the sort of thing Laura had been secretly saying to herself for the last few months.

And to tell the truth, Dante's declaration hadn't been entirely without effect. Oh, it still made her seethe to think of it, but somehow seeing Dante charging about rescuing Jet and torn up over his father's death had made Laura face up to her own loneliness. Visiting the nursing home with him, she had seen her mother as if through a stranger's eyes. She had realized just how much she didn't want to grow old alone.

And Dante did have his strong points, of course. His wit, his charm. There was nothing wrong with his mind, if he ever chose to use it on something. If he could just develop some kind of, of . . . structural integrity. A husband good enough for her would have to be capable of bearing more pressure than Dante could right now. He was too loose, too flimsy an aggregation of parts.

Although the materials were very promising. . . . After all, he loved her, didn't he? And for that matter, as she had wryly admitted to herself, he was very good-looking—which a potential mate should try to be, if at all possible.

Chop, chop, chop: vengefully Laura hacked up the bits of her already mutilated cabbage. "In case he hasn't told you," (chop) "Dante is quite convinced he's about to" (chop!) "die," she snapped. "I imagine that would put a hitch in any wedding plans."

Aunt Sophie absorbed this information. "Oh. So that's what he thinks, is it?" She nodded slowly to herself. Keeping her cigarette in her mouth, she rinsed her hands and then turned to bring a cake out of the refrigerator. "Lemon," she said, setting it on the scarred kitchen table to warm up. "Gwen's favorite. I made it yesterday."

"Yesterday . . . ?" Once again Laura felt the weight of Aunt Sophie's old gray eyes. "You knew," she said slowly. "You knew what was going to happen to Dante's dad."

Aunt Sophie shrugged. "I guessed." She returned to the stove and flipped her schnitzel over.

"Your coins," Laura said, remembering the stories Dante had told about his fortune-telling Hungarian aunt.

Wait— Had the coins shown Aunt Sophie something about Dante? About Dante and herself getting married, for instance? "I remember I was here last New Year's Eve and you were telling fortunes with them"—Laura frowned—"but you said everything was going to be great. You said it would be a wonderful year."

Aunt Sophie grunted. "So I lied. What the hell am I going to say on New Year's Eve, eh? What's the point in ruining a nice party?" She shook her head, and absent-mindedly tapped her cigarette ash into the kitchen sink.

"Couldn't you have done something? Sent him to the

hospital for a checkup or something?"

"Well, I thought about it, but then decided, Nah, hey—let the little bastard die," Aunt Sophie snapped.

Laura swallowed. "Sorry." Of course Aunt Sophie would have done everything she could to save her brother. Laura flushed and returned to her cabbage, although she had already reduced it to wafer-thin filaments.

"It's not so damn easy as all that. Oh, sure, when I was younger I used to think: Hell, I know what this means. I'd better jump in and straighten out Mary Furillo before she marries Jackson, the toad; or, I'll just tell Dante to let Jet do the sawing . . . but you can never be certain what the coins mean, heh? And the more you know, the less it seems you can do anything about it. And the worse the news, the less anybody listens. . . ." Sophie trailed off into silence. "I asked Anton about it once," she said at last. "Not in so many words, of course. He was always so smart. 'The Cassandra effect,' he called it."

She stopped, and took another drag on the cigarette between her shaking fingers. "There was nothing I could do," she said at last.

Nothing she could do. Not just about her little brother, Laura guessed, from the weary way she spoke the words. Nothing she could do about Anton, and Pendleton, and Jet, and all the tragedies of her long life.

Aunt Sophie stood at the stove, looking back in time. "When I was a girl, there wasn't any of this," she said. "My father could push a coin through your ear and pull it out your nose, but it was all a trick. That's what made it fun. Because when the magic is real, then all the rules

are gone. Nothing's safe anymore." She shook her head.
"We're lost. . . . Prophets and angels, charms and voodoo dolls and walk-aways and finger-spells: where the
hell is it going to end, heh? Look at Columbus, or Ma-
gellan: looking back, historians call you an explorer, but
at the time, you're just lost. We know so much, and we
can do so little. We learn all these secrets and they don't
help a damn."

"You know who you sound like?" Laura laid down
her knife and met Aunt Sophie's eyes square on. "You
sound just like Jet."

Well, that observation hadn't gone down too well, but
Laura was still thinking about it an hour later, after
lunch had been eaten and the dishes cleared away.

The whole family had this mythology about Jet, the
Outsider. The Changeling. And yet, to her eyes, he was
just as inextricably part of the family as Dante or Sarah
or Aunt Sophie herself. He had a room on the first floor,
just underneath Dante's. He had taken half the pictures
now hanging on the parlor wall: Dante sculling on the
river, Sarah at her graduation, the older Ratkays working
in the garden.

Consider the photograph of Mrs. Ratkay's cherished
Lombardy poplars. It was a black and white shot he must
have taken lying on his back, looking straight up into
their arms as they towered gracefully into a burnished
sky, their leaves glinting like coins. Obviously he had
taken it to please Gwendolyn. What difference was there,
really, between that photograph and the little clay pencil-
holder on the mantelpiece (too shallow to hold pencils
and so filled with mints left over from Halloween) that

Sarah had made her mum in her Grade 1 art class?

Really, the whole business made Laura itchy and impatient. At this very moment, according to Dante, Jet was out in the City, looking for the Sending he thought had stolen his soul. Why he was doing such an absurd thing when he should be at home feeling wretched with the rest of his family, Laura couldn't fathom. She could have kicked him. A family, a real family with brothers and sisters, aunts and uncles, old wars and stories and secrets: that was too precious a thing to abandon for the sake of a little personal growth.

Compounding her impatience was the uncomfortable feeling that she should really be at work. After finally deciding on a favorable orientation for Mr. Hudson's solarium, she had gone back to her initial plans and found to her dismay that there was something dead in them. Oh, the extension as she had sketched it was bright and airy and altogether attractive, but it seemed somehow . . . superficial.

The problem was, she didn't really know that much about Mr. Hudson. Here, now: essence of Ratkay was everywhere throughout this house. Jet's photographs and Dante's high-school baseball trophy; two posters advertising an old show of Sarah's rolled up and stashed behind a coat stand; the smell of borscht and fried onions; Gwendolyn's historical novels lying open on every other table; the imposing tallboy in the dining room filled with bottles of whisky and claret, gin and sherry and Tokay and good French wine. Like Scotch aging slowly in an oaken cask, Dante's family had aged together within these walls.

Dante's sister Sarah startled her, running down the

stairs and into the parlor. Her face was white and she was crying. "I need your help," she said.

Coming into Sarah's room, the first thing Laura thought was: bad luck, to sleep in a room with no mirrors.

There was a vast flowered Magyar quilt on the bed and a set of red-checked curtains that seemed vaguely ironic. A beautiful collection of dolls sat atop Sarah's dresser: an English girl with blue eyes and a porcelain face, a Spanish señorita with a black dress and a crimson fan, and a sharp-featured doll with the most incredible fall of copper-colored hair. A small pile of neatly folded clothing lay beside each of them, along with a selection of miniature combs, bows, ribbons, and barrettes.

"I heard the thump, thump, thump, from downstairs," Sarah said quietly. "I couldn't think what it could be, so I came up to look. When I was just outside the door, the thumping was louder and I could hear the bedsprings squeaking. It stopped as soon as I opened the door. That's what I saw."

A pair of muddy shoes lay discarded on the floor at the foot of the bed. They were dingy white canvas sneakers that had seen a lot of action. They might have fit an eight-year-old girl.

"A niece?" Laura suggested. "Cousin? Someone visiting for the funeral?"

"My daughter," Sarah said.

"I didn't know you—"

"I don't." Sarah closed her eyes. "It's just that we don't know anything about ghosts, you see. Even Dante hasn't got a clue. We were brought up as atheists, on moral grounds. But I can't deal with it anymore. Every time I turn around these days, she's there."

"Now, hold on," Laura began uneasily. She really didn't want Sarah to confide in her. "I don't know anything about ghosts either."

"You know more than we do," Sarah said fiercely. "I've heard Dante talk about it. The Chinese know what to do with angels. He told me you burn charms to appease your ancestors every day."

"Now, wait a minute," Laura said indignantly. "You make me sound like I just dropped off the boat from Easter Island."

"I mean it's obvious what's going on. It's just like a minotaur, only instead of fear conjuring a monster, it's guilt; it's my guilt coming back, but I *know* that already. The lesson's over. Class dismissed!" Sarah cried fiercely.

Laura winced. Despite her best efforts, she hadn't managed to dodge Sarah's secret. "You're being haunted by a ghost," she said, resigning herself.

"Not . . . haunted exactly," Sarah said. She glanced back at the shoes. "More like pestered."

Laura laughed. "At least she took off her shoes before bouncing on your bed!"

"Yeah." Sarah tried to grin. "I don't know where she learned her manners."

"Not from the father, I assume."

Sarah snorted.

Laura reached out to touch the red-haired doll; paused; looked to Sarah for permission.

Sarah nodded. "The father was slime. He had incredibly low standards for women, though, which at the time I confused with love. His condoms were bright green and glowed in the dark. I'm not kidding. I figured there might be trouble when I read the small print at the bottom of the package: 'Novelty Only. Do Not Use During Intercourse.' "

Guiltily Laura laughed.

Sarah sat on the edge of the bed, looking at the sweep of poplars outside her window. "Technically it was a miscarriage, but it might as well have been an abortion. Pro-life people think women don't care, you know that? They think we just toddle down to the clinic on a lunch break, whistle gaily to ourselves, and then hustle off to our next date." She touched the cameo pinned to the front of her vest. "Well it isn't like that. You don't forget."

Laura held the doll in her arms. She was strangely heavy, much heavier than Laura had expected. Her arms and legs didn't have the roly-poly quality so many dolls did; they were the wiry, active limbs of a two-year old. Her sharp nose tilted up at the end and there was mischief in her green glass eyes.

"It's not as if I'm stupid," Sarah pointed out. "I always knew what I was doing to myself. I kept track of how old she was. I worked out the day she would have been born—not just the due date, but a week later because the first child is usually late. I knew it was wrong to torment myself, but I had to do it. I deserved it. And every year when her birthday came around I always thought I should do *something*: put flowers on a grave, throw a party, get drunk. Something. Last year I had to do a show at Jokerz."

Laura looked at her.

Sarah almost smiled. "I was doing great, right up to the moment I spat on a guy in the front row."

Laura winced.

"And it's not as if it doesn't happen to ten thousand girls a year in this country. Or more," Sarah said restlessly. "God, that's the part that galls me. Who would have thought I'd be so bad at it? Me, of all people? I've always been tough, I've always been a fighter. And this wasn't even a real tragedy. I mean, it wasn't like Aunt Sophie, who lost her husband and her child when they were both real. There are women out there whose real flesh and blood children are hit by cars or kidnapped or, or whatever. They manage to go on. But I can't."

"You only see them from the outside," Laura said softly. She wondered what she had felt like, sitting in her mother's lap. "Even the most successful women have their ghosts."

"The whole idea of ghosts used to terrify me. Dante thought it was hilarious. He would tell ghost stories to me until Jet made him stop, and then I'd lie in bed at night with my eyes open and the light on for hours. Because it's what might have been, you see? It's unfinished business. It's death itself that scares Dante, but I figure if you go out with your accounts balanced, big deal. We're all going to buy it in the end. But to go out with something horribly wrong, to have that gnawing at you and gnawing at you . . ." Sarah closed her eyes.

Laura picked through the little box of doll accessories and took out a tiny tortoise-shell comb. Slowly she drew it through the doll's long auburn hair. Of course, it wouldn't be like this with a real child. A real child wouldn't sit so long. A real child would kick and squirm. But still.

"I know you aren't really an angel. But I have to do

something, you see. Mom really needs me now, but I'm no use to her like this. Obviously I could use a good strong dose of therapy, but I can't wait ten years to be functional again. I mean, God, what if Dante's right and he goes too? Who's going to hold this family together?"

Women, Laura thought. The women in the kitchen, chopping vegetables and crying.

Hair split heavily around the teeth of her toy comb like honey flowing, a river of it, stroke after stroke. Of course a real child might want to cut her hair short, or wear a baseball cap, or might be bald—you couldn't say. But still.

"So I need a, a charm, a ritual, anything. Something to ward her off, just for a few days. Something to lull my subconscious to sleep at least until the funeral is over. Then maybe I can find time. I mean, things can't go on like this; that's obvious."

But if she were sleeping, Laura thought, a real child might feel a little like this, resting in the bend of your arm. If she were sleeping, she might lean back like this while her mother combed her hair, one slow gentle stroke at a time. She would be warmer, of course. But still.

"I have to let go, I keep telling myself I have to let go—but it's easier said than done, you know?"

"Why?"

Sarah blinked. "Why what?"

"Why do you have to let go?" Gently Laura put the doll back on Sarah's dresser. Sarah was looking at her confusedly, like a woman suddenly woken from a dream.

"That's the trouble with you atheists," Laura contin-ued irritably. "You can't stop thinking about yourselves. I me mine, I did this, my subconscious, I'm torturing myself, blah blah blah." Laura nudged the pair of sneakers with her foot. "This doesn't have anything to do with you."

Sarah stared blankly at her. "What?"

Laura could have kicked her.

"You just don't get it, do you? *There is a ghost in the house!*" Laura cried. "Don't keep treating her as if she were just a bad dream, just something you made up. She's *real,* Sarah. Every bit as real as you are." Laura pulled her best Annoyed Oriental face. "You round-eyes are so stupid sometimes."

Sarah blinked. "So, uh . . . Okay, she's real. So, what am I supposed to do?"

"Find out what she wants and give it to her, I expect. Isn't that how you placate ghosts in the West?"

"How should I know what she wants?"

"Don't be coy," Laura snapped. "It's perfectly obvious what she wants."

Sarah's shoulders stiffened, then slowly sagged. "Me," she whispered. ". . . How am I supposed to give her that, Laura? I've already failed my one chance."

Laura shrugged. "Just be open, that's my advice. She'll let you know if she can." Laura grunted, nudging the sneakers once more. "I get the feeling she'll get what she wants, sooner or later."

Portrait

The monster in these pictures (dozens and dozens of them) stands just under six feet tall. Its teeth are small. Its talons are blunt. It is not roaring. In fact it was actually wheezing as I took these shots, but you can't tell that just from looking.

The monster in these photographs does not wear my soul on an amulet around its neck. It does not even wear a tie. The monster in these pictures wears a shabby, good-natured suit of cheap raw silk, worn at the cuffs.

The monster no longer wears his hair slicked back. Once black and gleaming with brilliantine, it is now gray and thin. Once the monster's smile was made of razors; now there's nothing there but a set of cheap false teeth.

Because Jewel's friend Albert, Confidence, the man who destroyed my life, who drove my father to suicide and turned my mother against me: when I finally met him face to face, he wasn't a monster anymore. He was a balding portly bookseller in a part of town that had been fashionable once but wasn't now. He was a decent guy, embarrassed by what he had been, sweating a little and smiling a lot.

And all I could do was shoot him, again and again, round after round, frame after frame.

It wasn't the camera that gave up at last. But my hands aren't made of plastic and steel, and they started shaking.

My eyes aren't glass, after all. Tears crawled from them, and I couldn't see.

Glass is a liquid. Laura learned that in an undergraduate course, looking at pictures of a cathedral seven hundred years old where the glass had run like a melting candle, leaving the windows thin at the top, thick and marbled at the bottom.

That thought, and remembering the feel of the doll cradled in her arms, and remembering the way the Ratkay home had made her own beautiful apartment seem so lonely: all those images swimming together in the hour of Ch'ou gave Laura the answer to the problem of Mr. Hudson's solarium. With a grunt she rolled over in bed, grabbed the notebook and pencil she kept on the night table and scribbled: WINDOWS.

She would find the windows from Mr. Hudson's first home, from the home he grew up in as a boy. She would use them, the same glass (maybe even the same frames, she hadn't decided yet), to wall in the solarium. Because no summer sky could be as beautiful as the one that floated over you as a child: no blue so deep, no clouds so majestic. No shade sifted through whispering leaves could ever be so mysterious.

But she would bring that back for him, she and Mr. Ling. Together they would make a place not only for the great man Hudson had become, but for the small boy he would always be.

There are a lot of ghosts in all of us, she thought— and fell asleep.

CHAPTER
FOURTEEN

PORTRAIT
I *have several pictures of Father's funeral, but the
one I come back to has no casket and no flowers.
Dante grabbed my camera and took it when the funeral
was over and we were back home, receiving condolence
calls. It's a quick shot, badly framed: Mother's back is
turned and I'm a little out of focus. Really, this is a picture of potato salad.*

Every day I read The New York Times; *it is the lens
through which I view the world. It is full of war and
poverty, atrocity and magic, glamours sinister and suspect. There is very little in it about potato salad. But
standing in the parlor the day of Father's funeral, feeling
the press of neighbors' hands, watching the dining table*

223

*disappear under home-baked pies and tubs of coleslaw
and casseroles wrapped in aluminum foil, that potato
salad seemed more real than the atrocities in* The Times:
as real as Dante. As real as Father's loss.

*I had not expected to stay all day in the front parlor,
but I did. I didn't say much, mind you. Stood silent,
mostly, watching our reflections meet and touch and pass
in Grandfather Clock's glass chest. But it was warm and
sad and human, and the quiet talk was better company
than silence; soothing as the wind whispering in the maple leaves, or the ceaseless murmur the river makes, singing its long way softly to the endless ocean.*

*When we die, are we nothing but a body, a broken
machine from which all meaning flies? Is a soul like
smoke, given off by the body's combustion, that wavers
and flees when the corpse grows cold?*

I thought so once.

*But meeting Albert, who had once been Jewel's Send-
ing, showed me I didn't understand much about souls.
About living. There was something more than mustard
and potatoes in that potato salad. There was a meaning
in that room that had everything to do with the food on
the table, and with Father, and with all of us who had
lost him. He was a part of all our lives, and he continued
in us even after he was dead.*

*I remember Aunt Sophie watching me, all that after-
noon. Her eyes were bloodshot from too many tears and
cigarettes. Of course, she had just lost the last living
member of her family. Edvard had died of fever, Leslie
was shot down during the War. Her father she lost to a
stroke in the summer of 1970, when the first minotaurs
were crawling out of Watts. Her mother died three years*

later. Pendleton committed suicide, of course.

Me she lost—or threw away—the week I was born.

Now little Anton had died too.

When I saw her watching me I expected something awful; a scene, threats, recriminations. That didn't happen. She just kept . . . looking at me. Once, I saw her talk to Sarah—a few phrases, nothing much—and afterwards I saw her slowly nod her head, looking at me. For a moment, I almost thought I saw something different in her eyes, a searching: as if, seeing me for the first time in thirty years, she had caught a glimpse of something she had never expected to see again.

Probably that was just my imagination.

That look doesn't show in this picture, of course. It's not really a very good photograph. When Dante gave it to me, I asked him why.

"Because you're in it," he said.

It was Friday, just after the funeral. The reception was still going on up at the house, but Dante was standing on the dock where he had cast his lure into the river a week before and reeled in a pike with a golden ring in its belly. He had not cried since his father collapsed beside the dining table. Mother had been devastated, Sarah's wide face blotched with tears; but Dante had not cried. Had felt very little, in fact. Puzzlement, maybe, that he was still alive.

He didn't think he had slept in the three days either, though it was difficult to remember. He felt dry and lifeless, not a man at all, but a leather puppet like the ones in Jewel's study.

Dante lived again the memory she had shown him:

three years old, the feel of his cheek against the carpet, the dust motes dancing, the relentless ticks of Grandfather Clock.

We live in time.

Our dreams go on forever, and our ambitions, and our hopes, and the great play of our ideas reaches for eternity.

But we live in time. We die in time.

It was twilight, and winter was coming on with the cold blue dusk. Shadows flowed down from the steep wooded sides of the river valley and crept over the water. Dante remembered lying chest down on a sheet of buckling ice, screaming for Jet. The dark water pulling, pulling.

He sat down on the end of the dock, his polished Italian shoes hanging over the dim water. The wooden planks creaked and rocked. Who was it who said we can never step in the same river twice? Diogenes? Father would know.

Father would have known.

He remembered his father's face in the bureau mirror one week ago, bending over the body lying there.

And like the touch of death, Dante felt the first hint of understanding. "Oh God," he whispered.

You have begun to guess what you have always known.

Jet, he thought desperately. Must get Jet.

Turning, he ran up the hillside, great frantic strides, tripping through the remains of Mother's garden, pulling the kitchen door open and shouting Jet's name.

The living room was dim and murmurous with condolences. On the dining table tall candles in polished sil-

ver candlesticks presided over trays of food brought over
by their friends and neighbors: lasagna and tuna casse-
role, bowls of potato salad, jelly salad, mashed potatoes
and coleslaw and poundcake and cherry pie and Corn-
ing-ware dishes wrapped in aluminum foil. Mother stood
pale and composed at the bottom of the table, accepting
sympathy.

Jet was standing with Mrs. Parret, the secretary at the
local school, listening to her with a strange kind of wonder. There was something in his face almost like grati-
tude.

Dante called his name. Whatever Jet saw, looking at
him, turned the uncharacteristic warmth in his eyes to
ashes.

"You've got to come with me," Dante gasped, dragging him from the room. People were staring at them,
Sarah too, distraught and murderous all at once, but he
didn't care; Christ, if what he guessed were true, there
was so much more to pay for than a disturbance at the
reception. "Get shovels," he cried breathlessly, pushing
Jet through the back door. "We've got to dig up the
body. Oh Jesus. Oh Jesus."

Jet looked at him, breath smoking in the twilight, face
pale beneath his ghastly birthmark. "Okay. Okay," he
said, catching Dante's panic.

Together they raced down to the boathouse.

It was dark by the time they reached the island. Jet
crouched by the graveside, shining a flashlight into the
pit. Dante dug like a madman, heedless of the mud spattering the expensive new suit he'd bought for the funeral.
The blade of his shovel struck something firmer than

dirt. Flinging it aside, he used his hands, crouching by the head of the grave, scooping out the cold black earth until his cuffs were black and his dirty fingers were stiff and numb. The body had begun to putrefy. The stink of it clung to him, wrapped around the smells of cold mud and leaves. Under the flashlight's weak beam, pale as moonlight, Dante's hands slowed, brushing dirt from the corpse's face, smoothing its thin hair, cleaning mud away from its sunken eyes.

"Oh my God," Jet whispered.

"I knew it. I knew it all the time," Dante said dully. Gently he brushed the dirt from his father's thin lips. Gently he closed the lids of his father's old blue eyes, empty now in death.

"What do you mean, you knew?" Jet asked, some time later.

"It was his body. It was his body on the bureau. It was his body we opened up and I knew it, I knew it. But I wouldn't let myself know."

Slowly Jet nodded. "And that shaped what we saw."

"I'm the angel. Remember? . . . I knew he was going to die, I knew it all along. But I wouldn't tell myself. I could have saved him, but I didn't."

"It's a new world," Dante said. "Magic isn't just a few psychos having visions. It's real. In a few more years it will be realer than everything else." He stroked the thin hair on his father's forehead. He thought, I get it, Jewel. I finally really get it.

"Listen," Jet said. "I mean, should we . . . ?" He nodded awkwardly at Dante's discarded shovel.

"Not yet."

"Okay."

Dante remained sitting by the grave edge, dry as dust. Empty. He straightened the cuffs on his slacks. Pulled up his socks.

Jet turned off the flashlight and stood up. "Moon's coming up early," he observed. "Full, pretty much."

Dante didn't answer.

"Christ, it's cold," Jet said. "Wish I'd thought to grab a coat."

"Take mine."

"You'll freeze."

"No, seriously. I can't feel it," Dante said. He stood and gave Jet his charcoal-gray suit jacket. It was a heavy wool blend, subtly veined with dull red threads that picked up the garnets in his cuff links.

"Thanks," Jet said.

"I tracked down Confidence yesterday, after the reception," Jet remarked, some time later. Dante didn't comment. "You know what he said, about winning my soul from Pendleton?—'Worst deal I ever made.' That's what he said." From out of the darkness, Dante heard Jet's soft dry laugh. "Talk about disillusioning."

Dante could barely feel anything: cold, grief, guilt. But he discovered he was glad, to hear Jet's cool voice coming out of the darkness.

"Turns out every Sending gets a soul. Once you're in the world, you're real; that's what Confidence said. Like a sandbar in a river: a soul just silts up against you. After a few years, Confidence had to live for more than the hustle. Started betting on baseball, then fell in love with the sport. Kept the box scores from all the Red Sox games, made lousy bets on them, hoping they would win. Met a nice girl. Settled down. Two kids. Hey presto: a life. And hey presto, a soul to go with it."

Dante blinked. "That means you must have had one too."

"Yeah."

Jet swung his foot; Dante heard the sound of it, scuffing aimlessly in the leaves. " 'I have no soul, I am different, I am not human; Dante must do all the living while I stay in the shadows and watch.' "

"I never forced you to."

"But those were the rules," Jet said. "I made them up myself."

He shrugged. ". . . We do not make these choices with our faculties complete. I was two weeks old when I decided you were the only thing that mattered. By three years I was a satellite more fixed to you than the moon is to the earth. . . . By fifteen, of course, I was aware of your limitations as a god," Jet added wryly. "Your obtuseness, your maddening refusal to see."

"I had my reasons for not looking," Dante said grimly.

"Your neglect." Jet paused. ". . . But the die was cast, there was no going back. I had cried out for a king and gotten a log; it has happened before."

After a while he said, "Later on, when she was wiser, Jewel's were the best Sendings. That's what Confidence said. Other Sendings might take years to work out from under their angel's preconceptions. Jewel birthed hers with the fewest strings attached. But Confidence was her first, and it seemed like a fine thing, to play for the soul of a firstborn son. . . ."

Dante said, "I must have known for years that Dad was sick. For years. Ever since the body started growing under the blanket on my dresser."

Still low on the horizon, the moon cast a spectral light over the river valley; just enough for Dante to catch a dim blur when Jet gestured with his hands. Just enough to show Jet's thin shape beneath the willow tree, a shadow moving against a backdrop of shadows. "I mean, good Lord! The prospect of actually having to live a life, instead of simply scrutinizing you ridiculous humans through *The New York Times*! Now I must decide, do I like blues or jazz? Detective novels or spy thrillers? Imagine: to be reduced to coming to you—ugh!—for advice about women!—The whole concept is terrifying."

"Whole new worlds to brood about," Dante agreed.

Jet sighed. "It's not a very attractive habit, brooding, but I am good at it. I give myself credit for that."

"I can't stand it," Dante announced.

"I beg your pardon?"

Fiercely Dante turned back to the grave. He began flinging the dirt off his father's body, throwing it in ferocious handfuls into the darkness. The bandage on his right hand was black with mud. "I can't stand it. I will not allow this." He leaned over the grave and shouted into it. *"Do you hear me, Jewel!"*

Jet returned to the grave, put a hand on Dante's shoulder. "Hey," he murmured. "Easy does it."

"Do you hear me, Jewel! Bring it on, angel. Bring on your god. I have my hand over my dead father's face,

you witch, you madwoman. You want me to look? Well I'm *looking*!"

Hunching over he yelled into his father's lifeless face. "I'm the fucking Resurrection Man, god damn it, and I'm coming to get you!" He grabbed the corpse and pulled its shoulders free of the earth, shaking it in fury from side to side. "Wake up! Wake up, you son of a bitch! I'm talking to you!"

"Dante! Get a hold of yourself!"

Dante whirled, clubbing Jet hard across the face with the back of his hand. "Leave me alone," he hissed.

(And deep, deep inside himself he raised the scissors off Jewel's desk. *You don't want this,* Jewel whispered, eyes black and steady as gun-barrels.

"Fuck you," Dante said. And plunged the scissors into her neck.

A storm of colored wings burst around him.)

As he stared at his father's corpse in its shallow grave, the long incision down its chest split open. Spiders streamed out.

"Oh my God," Jet said weakly, grabbing the flashlight. Hundreds of black bodies jerked and scuttled under its pale beam. Thousands of thin black legs.

Dante felt himself tearing apart like a wet paper towel, all the scar tissues of his life ripping open, spilling out the secrets he had tried so hard not to see. Jet's loneliness ran out of him like blood, and Sarah's dreadful pain, all stringy hair and savage wit. Grandma Ratkay, pawing at his shirt, and the blind panic as he tried to pull away from her, she stank so much of coming death. The arguments between his parents; the time Anton called his wife a bitch when he didn't think the kids could hear.

And spilling out too, the thousand memories of his father weary, coughing, incomprehensibly small and tired, his neat hands trembling, and I knew, Dante thought. Oh, God, I knew it all along.

Jewel's god gushed up inside Dante and filled his lungs, fountained from his fingertips, his nipples, the ends of his hair; blinded him, spilling from his eyes. It moved through Dante like a hurricane blowing through an empty shirt, distending him, whipping him senselessly this way and that. Dante fell flat, stunned. A ragged, heartbroken sound whispered out of the darkness. It was Jet, sobbing. He too lay blasted on the ground.

Jewel's god poured into the dead body of Dante's father, filling it up, opening its eyes, speaking through its mouth. *You called me,* it said. *I have come.*

Years passed.
What do you want?
Dante was breaking apart. Now the dreadful secrets were crawling out of him, about Duane the bully and Jet, Mrs. Farrell and his father dying dying dead. He felt his hands twitch and tremble, beginning to detach themselves from his wrists, starting to scuttle into the darkness.

His whole body was crawling, shivering, breaking into spiders.

Unimaginably distant, his light voice ragged and fraying, Jet laughed at the god in Dr. Ratkay's body. "I think you should know we were raised atheists," he whispered. "—On moral grounds."

Jet screamed. With angel's eyes Dante saw the butterfly tear from his cheek and circle in the air. A few drops of blood fell from its twisting wings.

"Oh, Jet," Dante whispered. To Jewel's god he croaked, "I want my father."

Your father is in Hell.

"Then take me there."

Dr. Ratkay's body smiled gravely. *The descent to Hell is the same from every place.*

And then Jewel's god was gone. In the deafening silence Dante lay sprawled over his father's grave, flat as veins empty of blood. He could see Jet's body, a lump of shadow in the moonlight a few feet away.

"Jet?"

"Unh."

"Jet? You okay?"

"Definitely not." Jet groaned. He gathered himself slowly together, each gesture brittle and hesitant, as if testing for broken bones.

"Hey," Dante said, starting to move.

"Hey what?"

"Shit, ouch. I've got something in my hand. Ouch." Gingerly Dante opened the bandaged right hand that had been lying on his father's face. Something glimmered there: little barbs of moonlight. "Hey. It's the lure."

"The lure?"

"Yeah. You know. The one I used to find Pendleton's thumb. I wonder what I'm supposed to do with it."

Jet experimented with breathing, seeing how much air he could take in before his ribs hurt. "Just out of curiosity, Dante—not meaning to intrude—but are you going to have another crazy fit any time in the near future?"

Gingerly Dante sat up, cupping the lure carefully in his right hand. "I'd have to say the odds favor it."

Jet grunted. "Great." Dante saw him reach up to touch his face. "Ow. Hey." He fumbled for the flashlight, found it, turned it on himself. "Hey. Dante."

Dante whistled. Lit from below, Jet's sharp face appeared positively diabolical: knife-blade cheeks, thin mouth, obsidian eyes glinting beneath ferocious brows. But where the birthmark had been, only a faint cobweb of white lines remained, like threads of scar tissue. "The butterfly's gone."

Jet flicked off the flashlight. "Damn."

"I thought you hated it."

"I hate you sometimes too, but I wouldn't want to lose you." Even in the dark, Dante could imagine Jet's quick grin. "I've become accustomed to my face. Anyway, if you don't know what to do now—with the lure I mean—you're not your father's son." In Father's Declamation Voice he chanted:

" 'But I myself sat on guard, bare sword in hand, and prevented any of the feckless ghosts from approaching the blood before I had speech with Tiresias.' "

"Oh," Dante said. "Oh. I see." He looked from the barbed lure in his hand to his father's body, lying crookedly in the grave.

Now that he had begun to recover from having touched Jewel's god, he realized there was something different inside himself. The little web within his breast was gone, and Jewel's study with it. Instead, Jewel whispered through him everywhere, fluttering through his veins and arteries, beating in slow time to the rhythm of his lungs, crawling under his eyes and inside the ringed bones of his vertebrae. There was a sort of weightlessness inside him, like the quality he had sensed in Tristan Chu: a wind of possibility. He looked from lure to body and saw a channel there. I am become a riverbed, he thought giddily. I am become a stream.

A thread of panic checked him, remembering Jewel's study carpeted in butterflies, her blouse seething and her empty nylons. Wasn't that what he had always feared, that to loose the angel in him would drive him mad? And it hadn't been a stupid fear, damn it. It wasn't just cowardice; the danger was real. The angel touch had taken even Jewel in the end; broken her into a madness with a million heaving wings.

"Jet?"

"Yeah?"

"I don't want to go crazy."

"Okay."

"I don't want to end up like Jewel." Remembering the way his hands had started to twitch and scuttle, breaking into spiders.

"We'll use the buddy system," Jet said, hefting the flashlight. "First sight of lunacy, I'll lay you out cold."

Dante winced. "Ouch. Thanks."

"No problem," Jet assured him. "Am I not my brother's keeper?"

Slowly Dante closed his bandaged right hand around the fishing lure, feeling the barbs bite into his tender palm. Pain welled up in him, pushing through his hand, reaching back down his arm, through his shoulders and inside the cage of his ribs, piercing at last into the secret places of his heart.

He remembered his father, robed in pipe smoke, writing letters with his cherished Waterman, scratching away, his right elbow brushing the skull on his desk.

Remembered him standing at the dinner table, glass upheld and full of pale gold, smiling and drinking a Hippocratic toast.

Remembered him weeding in the garden with Mother, narrow back bending, the broad brim of his gardening hat shadowing his eyes.

There was a river building up in Dante, a hot, insistent pressure that made his throat cramp and his jaws ache. It beat dully behind his eyes, until finally he couldn't stand it anymore, he couldn't hold it back, and a sob tore through him, making his shoulders heave helplessly, twisting his pale face with grief.

A drop of blood squeezed between Dante's fingers and fell onto his father's cold lips.

Tick.

The trees had gone vaporous and pale, their branches made of moonlight. The dark wind began to murmur and sigh. Willow fronds trailed and twisted, light as moonshine.

From across the grave, Jet stirred. "Hell is shot in black and white," he muttered.

Tock.

Another drop of blood spotted his father's lips. Forceless, unfelt, the wind from the dead lands rose: sighs and mutters, moans and laments.

At long last Dante was crying. Tears welled out of him; he felt himself losing shape, dissolving into them, like a riverbank crumbling in a flood. He was nothing, he was tears, he was a riverbed of grief.

Tick, tock, tick: blood spattered onto his father's face. "Come back," Dante whispered. "Please come back."

Tears streamed from his hand.

The babbling wind rose.

(And his daddy held him in his arms, swinging him breathless like an angel over the snow and he was laughing he was laughing it was forever, forever, forever.)

"Come on, god damn you." The pain in Dante's hand was unbearable. He wanted to scream. "Come on, come on, I summon you, my father, Anton Ratkay, healer, wise man, pipe-smoker, French wine drinker, god damn you. I summon you and your Greek quotations and your Beethoven quartets. I summon you, Father; I summon you, angel of death. I summon you, dead man! Dead man! Dead man, I bring you back. —Daddy? Daddy, come here. *Come back!*"

Anton Ratkay opened his eyes.

". . . Dante?" he whispered. Droplets of blood fell and vanished like seconds on his dead lips. Dante had recalled him, summoned him like a cold wind issuing from the bottomless well of Death.

It came to Dante with sudden, shocking clarity that he had nothing to say.

His soul swelled huge within his breast, but he couldn't break it into words. God damn it, he had nothing to say,

and all he could do was cry, watching his tears and blood
fall pattering onto his father's corpse.

"Dante?" his father said again. His filmy eyes rolled
back and forth like the eyes of the almost blind. (Like
the eyes of Sally Chen in Seven Cedars Nursing Home,
dim with cataracts, that could not see her daughter in
Laura, but lingered on her, anguished, unrecognizing.)

"Thirsty," his father said. His voice was thin and faint,
like the wind blowing through withered grass on a cold,
cloudy day. Blood fell onto his gray lips; darkened; then
dried, like raindrops falling on parched earth.

Dante cried with frustration, raging at himself for his
own stupid silence. But what was there to say to a man
who had sired him, raised him, cut him down, praised
him, rebuked him, fed him, ignored him, loved him?

Thank you?

I'm sorry?

"You *left*," Dante cried.

Dr. Ratkay, gathering strength, gazed at his son. " 'At
birth our death is sealed, and our end is consequent on
our beginning.' "

"Don't *quote*," Dante yelled, furious. "I didn't call you
up to talk to some dead Roman, I called for you. For
you! The Romans are dead: all dead, you hear me? But
we're alive. I'm alive, Jet's alive and now you're alive too.
I brought you back." Dante grabbed his father's shoulders. He stopped with a gasp as the forgotten lure dug
once more into the palm of his hand.

Dr. Ratkay cried out as Dante's blood spilled waste-
fully on the ground. The dead wind rose, and dim shapes
clouded around them: Grandmother Ratkay, smelling of

talcum powder and flower-scented soap; and another figure, riddled with small holes, dragging a parachute behind him, its silk lines like a tangle of spiderweb.
"Leslie?" Dr. Ratkay whispered.

(The great willow murmured, its thick limbs creaking.
A curtain of fronds settled whispering around Jet, en-
closing him. "Pendleton," he breathed.)

A little girl in a baseball cap elbowed in close, sucking
at Dante's arm. He felt ice spread through his veins at
the touch of her mouth.

"What's going to happen to Mother?" Dante said
fiercely through his tears. "Or Sarah? Or any of us? What
if someone gets sick? Who's going to choose the wine?"

"I'm sorry," his father said. "I did the best I could."

Hot tears were pouring down Dante's cheeks. "I failed
you."

"We all fail," his father said. "That's a great secret,
Dante. Nobody tells you that. Sooner or later we all fail
at everything important." His face was losing its color
once again, and his voice, which had strengthened, was
fading, breaking up like a swirl of fading pipe smoke.
"We fail our wives, our friends, our children," he whispered.

"How can you bear it?" Dante said, crying, pressing
his face against his father's face, his tears wet on his father's cheek, the smell of pipe smoke and dusty carpet everywhere, the smell of dust drifting and falling, falling.
"What am I supposed to do?" he cried. "Dad? Dad?
What am I supposed to do?"

The old man's eyes had closed. With the last of his
strength he gripped Dante's hand. "Live," he sighed.

Tick tick tick.

                        *   *   *

Tick.

Tick.

"But I *can't*," Dante cried.

Scrabbling to his knees, he leaned over his father's grave. "Come back. You live then, you traitor." Wildly he pulled the lure out of his hand and slashed at his wrist with the barbs. "I am the Resurrection and the Life, god damn it! I am God and I command the dead and you may not leave." A stream of blood spurted from his arm. Ice closed instantly around it as the gray dead surged in on him. "You made me, you bastard! You can't walk out on me now. You stay here and fight. You go back to the house and apologize to Mother this instant. I am God and you will do what—"

Pain exploded across Dante's face and he fell back, stunned.

. . . Then blood was welling from a split lip and his teeth were aching. His head rang and there were tears on his face.

He felt sick.

"Sorry," Jet said. He hefted the flashlight and then dropped it on the ground.

Dante threw up.

Jet hunkered down beside him and squeezed his wrist hard to stop the bleeding. "But you were getting a little out of control."

The real world was back; all the shadows were dense and solid once again. Dante heard a plop as something slipped into the river. A marten, maybe. His hand really hurt and he found he was shivering. "It's okay," he said.

And later, "Thanks."

"I'm c-c-cold!" a third voice complained.

Dante and Jet both yelped in surprise.

A young girl huddled next to them in the gloom. Her head had been tucked under her arms, as if in fright; somehow they had overlooked her completely. Now she sat up, shivering, in jeans and a T-shirt. She wore a baseball cap, catcher's style, with the bill turned backwards. She squinted as Jet turned the flashlight on her.

"Who are you?"

"I don't know," she said, hugging herself miserably. "I wanted to get back to my mom, so I followed you."

In the flashlight's beam, Dante saw that her mouth was wet and stained with blood. "The ghost," he murmured. Remembering her freezing lips, he pulled his bloody arm protectively into his body. "Only she isn't a ghost anymore."

"Sarah," Jet murmured, wonder in his voice. "You're Sarah's little girl. What's your name?"

"I don't know," the girl said irritably. "I think it starts with a J. Boy, it sure is cold," she repeated, staring hungrily at the suit jacket Jet was wearing. The two of them locked eyes.

Exasperated, Jet grunted and made Dante compress his own wound. ("Ow! Shit," Dante swore.) With no great grace Jet doffed Dante's suit jacket and wrapped it around the ex-ghost.

"Thanks," she said. "So—how about some food?"

"Oh, certainly! Anything else?" Jet growled.

Dante didn't move. "He's dead."

"Un-hunh."

"Really dead." Two or three more tears ran down Dante's face unheeded. Leftovers. "I couldn't bring him back."

"He wouldn't come," Jet said. He pointed to Sarah's daughter. "She made it. She wanted to come, and she came."

"I'm hungry," the girl repeated, in case someone might have missed it the first time.

Dante nodded. "We should cover him up." He rose unsteadily to his feet, feeling faint and sick and aching in altogether too many places. The blood on his forearm was clotting. He saw the lure where it had fallen on the ground and kicked it into his father's grave. "Not . . . not the greatest tool for cutting your wrists," he muttered.

Jet looked at him for a long moment, then burst out laughing.

And Dante laughed too, snuffling through his cut lip and bloody nose, feeling grief and hilarity swirling inside him like the Glenlivet his father used to give him when they went out hunting. Something else was in there too, now: a flight of butterflies. A stream of possibilities. "I have become an angel after all," he murmured. "I am become a riverbed."

Jet's shaggy eyebrows rose. "Let's go put you to bed, bed. You too," he growled at the girl, not unkindly. Swiftly he stooped and picked the lure out of Dr. Ratkay's grave. "You touched God, Dante. You walked through the valley of the shadow of death and returned. I think, this time, you'd better take a walk-away. Don't you?"

Reluctantly Dante nodded. "I guess I'm not an atheist anymore." And glancing at his father's grave he added, "One more disappointment for you, Dad."

In ten minutes of hard work they covered up Dr. Ratkay's body. "Goodbye," Dante said, lingering by the grave. "You may have failed, but you succeeded too, you know. Succeeded in everything." He wanted to say something else, find more words. Dredge up a classical epitaph worthy of his father, maybe.

But the night was cold, and Sarah's girl was shivering.

"Not much point bringing her from beyond the grave if you let her catch her death of cold," Jet remarked; and so Dante nodded, and shuffled towards the boat.

Jet started to follow with the girl, then stopped, retraced his steps, and picked up the flashlight. Thoughtfully he gave its steel shaft an experimental heft. He darted a quick glance at Dante, considering his bloody nose and split lip. "You know, I've always wanted to do that."

"I'll bet!" Dante laughed painfully. "Was it as good as you thought it would be?"

"Not bad," Jet allowed. "Not bad at all."

EPILOGUE

AS I WRITE THIS I AM SITTING IN THE FORT WE BUILT
on Three Hawk Island. Warm soft summer sur-
rounds me, and the low throb of cicadas makes
the air shake and sigh; makes the willow fronds twist and
untwist before me.

Soon I will have to row back across the river to the
house. Dante and Laura are waiting. There's a wedding
rehearsal planned for three, and it would be in poor taste
for the best man not to attend. So, I must leave my fort
in the willow tree, the hidden place where I am king, and
go once more to stand on the outskirts of Dante's life; to
smile and make polite applause.

Who knows? Perhaps next year it will be me, walking
down the aisle. The magic is rising all the time; life is

short, but full of possibilities. And if I do find a mate for my strange heart . . . will she be dour and deliciously jaundiced, an expert at *The Times* crossword puzzle? Or a broad-shouldered blonde in hiking boots to help me escape into a wilder life of clouds and rivers?

If I do marry, I'll get the better of the bargain, for Dante will make far funnier speeches at my wedding than I could ever make at his.

Portrait

When I took my most important portrait, I thought I was only shooting a landscape. Such are the ironies of life!

It was late on a summer's day much like this one. I had started out to give the fort another coat of waterproofing, but the magic of the afternoon entrapped me. I pulled up the western blind and sat on the rail with my back against a big branch and one leg swinging lazily in space. Below me the river split and hurried foaming around the tip of Three Hawk Island. A mild summer breeze lazed through the air; thin willow leaves slowly turned and twisted like charms on a green bracelet; bamboo chimes thin as birds' bones clicked together and swung apart, singing snatches of a summer song. A delicious smell of wood and mud and water rose from the eddy beneath my feet, and sunlight dripped like honey down the willow fronds.

By chance—or maybe fate—I had a roll of color film in my camera. Clambering down on impulse, I took the runabout and put-putted fifty yards upstream. Then, drifting with the river's current, I focused on the great, green, melancholy willow and took this shot. You can just see the huge branches spreading out behind waterfalls of twisting green; midway up and a little to the left a red-lacquer pagoda peeks through, our fort. It could just as easily be a trysting place for lovers, perhaps; or the hermitage of an ancient sage.

Overhead, vast unknowable clouds build and dissolve in a vaster sky, deep summer blue.

I didn't know it was a portrait until much later.

Two hundred years of life: according to Dante, that's what Pendleton was playing for when he laid down his faked full house, aces over eights. Confidence paid a cheat with a cheat, I guess. Year after year the willow's black roots pierced and encircled my father's body, drawing him into themselves, making him part of the tree. No doubt he'll get his two hundred years.

I do not think trees live in time as we do; they last too long.

Time changes things. Pendleton's mistake when he cheated at cards, or Dr. Ratkay's death: at first, such things seem devastating, losses that will cripple you forever.

Time passes.

The branch broken withers and dries. New limbs branch into the emptiness where the old bough flourished. In three years, or five, what was a mutilation has become only a landmark, and a pattern of growth.

A man lives in his eyes, glinting and skipping over the surface of his days, spinning down the stream of time, each moment in the grip of a changing current, a different eddy; dazzled by the play of light on water.

A tree stands still. Time moves slowly, for it lives at the roots of things; any lesson that takes less than years to teach is difficult for a tree to grasp. Grief lingers, and the ache of loss: those things don't change. But seeping into every leaf, a little guilt burns away each autumn, and falls, spinning down the river. Winter's long sleep begins, and with each spring the tree wakes knowing mercifully less than it did the year before.

I have always loved the great willow. I love to lie in the fort and listen to its sighs and silences, its long slow melancholy. . . .

Beyond the southern window of the fort there is such a glory of sun and shifting leaves this summer day I have to squint, dazzled, and turn away. Leaf-shadow twists and untwists in my little wooden room. Cicadas sing. The river runs and runs below; and despite myself I am content, if only for a little while.

For was it not a thousand days my father held me after all?

Did he not rock me to sleep a thousand times in his strong arms?